Cries in the Night

CRIES IN THE NIGHT

Elsie W. Strother

AVALON BOOKS
THOMAS BOUREGY AND COMPANY, INC.
NEW YORK

© Copyright 1985 by Elsie W. Strother
Library of Congress Catalog Card Number: 85-91256
ISBN 0-8034-8534-4

PRINTED IN THE UNITED STATES OF AMERICA
BY HADDON CRAFTSMEN, SCRANTON, PENNSYLVANIA

Cries in the Night

Chapter One

Dr. Pitt was holding Alison Munro's hand. He meant to be comforting with his fatherly gestures, she supposed, but he made her nervous instead.

Suddenly the heavyset doctor let go of her hand and gently patted her shoulder. Assuming a smile, he said, "You'll be just fine, my dear. All you need is complete rest, good nourishing food, and clean air. You're far too thin, you know."

"Thank you, Doctor. I'll try to rest and eat a lot when I'm home again. And the air down in Aiken is very good."

"South Carolina is hardly the place to

1

recover from a lung infection, Alison. Your father knew that one should listen to one's doctor. And if he had only followed my advice more—"

Alison interrupted him. "Your advice came too late, I'm afraid." A chill skittered the length of her spine. She didn't want to be reminded of her beloved father's recent decline from a specimen of ruddy good health to a pitiful shadow of himself.

"Mrs. Stevens did all she could for him, Alison dear. She mourned his death as did all of us."

"Oh, I know. Everybody was so kind. And you especially, Doctor, went out of your way to be thoughtful."

"Tut, my dear, I was as fond of your father as I am of you." He patted her shoulder again. "I want you to spend a few weeks at the Honoria Nursing Home. Honoria Stevens will take great care of you, and I can keep an eye on your progress."

"I—I don't want to go there. That's where Daddy spent his last days, and I don't want to be reminded."

"I know, dear, I know. But it's best for you. Believe me, honey." He squeezed her shoulder.

Alison didn't want to heed him, but she was feeling forlorn and scared. She needed to trust someone, and all her summer friends had already left Fairview. Besides, the doctor knew much more about medical matters than she did.

"All right," she murmured, "I'll go to the nursing home, but only till I feel strong enough to make the trip back to Aiken."

"That's a good girl! You know how beneficial the sea air is. Now what have you done about your family's summer cottage?"

"Nothing. I really haven't done much of anything except take an indefinite leave of absence from my teaching job."

"Just as well. You can arrange everything when you're better. Now you go gather up your belongings at the cottage and drive straight out to the nursing home. Meanwhile, I'll telephone Honoria Stevens to let her know you're on your way. I'll tell her to take extra special care of you."

"Thank you, Doctor."

The need to cry was like a bubble inside Alison's chest, getting bigger and bigger until she either let go with sobs or exploded. She did neither. She gritted her teeth as she drove to the summer cottage that had once been the scene of so much love and fun. It had lacked her pretty mother the last few years—cancer had taken her—but even so Alison's father and she had managed to enjoy getting away from the Carolina heat by themselves to bask in the cool of coastal Maine. Yet now the small white house seemed very desolate.

It took Alison only a few minutes to throw a few necessities into a suitcase, lock the cottage securely, and take off for the Honoria Nursing Home.

It was a fifteen-minute drive from the tiny town of Fairview, following the rugged coast all the way. When at last the weathered gray structure came into view, Alison had a moment of foreboding. The nursing home had never been a welcoming sight, not even at the height of summer. Now, in autumn, it seemed rather like a fairy-tale ruin filled with creaks and groans and rattles and cobwebs.

Witches might feel at home in it, Alison thought. Then she had to smile at her silly fancies. After all, her father had been well taken care of there, had seemed comfortable and reasonably content, had talked of going horseback riding again when they returned to Aiken.

She struggled to quell a choking feeling and tried to stifle the sobs that threatened to explode with the force of a breaker.

The sun, nearly blocked by heavy charcoal clouds, was sending thin, weak rays through the chilly sky. It was a somber sky. A cold, cold sky.

"My dear!" Honoria Stevens exclaimed when she greeted Alison at the door. "I'm so glad to see you again, although I'm sorry that your own sickness has brought you back." Her smile was so tight, it seemed to be stitched in place, and her six feet of solid strength were rather intimidating.

"I'm not sick," Alison said. "It's just that I've been under a strain, and Dr. Pitt said I had a spot on my lung. It's nothing, really.

All I need, he said, was rest and good air."

Mrs. Stevens's hair was dyed a pinkish red, her eyes were like polished steel, and her voice was like the rest of her—manufactured. Alison had met her before, of course, but the tall woman appeared different now. Alison warned herself that she must not be hasty in her appraisal. Mrs. Stevens might be the soul of genuine tenderness.

"Sam will carry your gear to your room, dear. You remember Sam?"

"Hello," Alison said to the big handyman.

His smile and his murmured "Miss Munro" were friendly.

She followed Sam up a long flight of steps and into a large corner room, one side of which faced the ocean. The windows were open, and a chilling breeze whipped inside.

"Let's close the windows, Sam, shall we?" Alison suggested.

"Sorry, Miss Munro, but fresh air is part of the therapy here, you know."

"But surely not to the point of freezing to death," she said.

He smiled at her exaggeration. "I'll close them if Miss Honoria says it's okay."

Alison wasted no time before running downstairs and knocking on the door that opened on Mrs. Stevens's private quarters.

"Come in," the woman said.

The room was warm and frilly-feminine. Everything was pink and ruffly. A less likely abode for the redoubtable Honoria Stevens could not be imagined.

"Mrs. Stevens, my room is too cold to be tolerated," Alison said bluntly. "Sam won't close the windows without your permission."

"You know, dear, that many of our patients have lung problems, and cool, fresh air is a must!"

"Fresh, I can understand, but freezing—"

"Tell Sam I said an exception can be made in your case. Until Dr. Pitt tells me different, I'll spoil you a bit. He's due to make his rounds in the morning."

Alison became aware she was being treated as someone special when she found she had a private bathroom. Most of the patients had sinks in their rooms but had to share the other facilities.

Now that her windows were closed, she began to make herself at home. She saw the bathroom had evidently not been used for some time. The various faucets emitted a variety of noises—belches, rumbles, and gurgles—before they finally allowed a trickle of rusty water to flow.

Her door suddenly burst open and a youngish woman in a nurse's uniform came in with a cup of bouillon.

"Here we are," she cried heartily. "Our nice little cup of nourishment. I'll put it on the table."

"Don't you ever knock before entering?" Alison asked, holding her irritation at bay.

"Why, no. I'm the nurse, you know. I'm Nola Brown and I'm used to seeing everything. It's no use hiding away from me!"

"I'd like some privacy, if you don't mind," Alison said softly. "It's not that I'm hiding anything, but please knock before coming in from now on, won't you?"

This nurse was new. Perhaps she didn't know better. She gave Alison a peculiar look, failed to answer, and left quickly.

Alison gazed out the side window. The pines in the distance threw restless shadows over the brown earth. It was a dismal view, but Alison was feeling more content. She could take pleasure in looking at the ocean crashing on the rocks below from her other window. She was pleased that she'd gotten her way about closing the windows and that she'd straightened out the overeager nurse. She must straighten herself out, too, and try to get over her recent loss. Life must go on and she must face it.

The bouillon stayed untasted on the table. She could not make herself swallow anything that had fat floating in small globs on its surface. She emptied the cup down the drain and had another moment of triumph. No bossy nurse was going to get the better of *her!*

Fully unpacked and somewhat rested, Alison made her way downstairs. As she passed Mrs. Stevens's door, she was surprised to hear her own name spoken.

"I suppose that Alison girl inherited her father's estate," Honoria was saying.

A masculine voice answered. "Yes, the

Munro holdings are substantial, I believe.
You couldn't know that it was all tied up
in trust funds for the daughter, could you,
when you nursed her father?"

Alison recognized Dr. Pitt's voice. The
nursing home evidently liked to inquire
into the monetary status of its patients.
In a way it was not surprising since their
charges were so high. Alison and her father had joked that a stay at the Honoria
Nursing Home was as expensive as a
Mediterranean cruise.

She was walking toward the front porch
when Honoria's door opened and the
voices became even clearer.

"This Joseph Lansing I told you about,"
the doctor said briskly, "is a young man,
wealthy I'm told, and suffering from nervous exhaustion. You'll find—"

Alison had opened the front door and
heard no more.

The sea was blue and green, violet and
amethyst, streaked with pale ribbons of
wandering currents. From the porch she
couldn't see the waves crashing against
the dark rocks, but she knew if she went
to the edge of the cliff she could look down
on the ferocity of the breakers.

Sitting on a rocking chair, gazing at the sea, with its surging power, its foaming pulse, Alison felt very much alive. And she knew she was recovering from her tragic loss.

A large brown dog ran up to her, tail wagging, tongue lolling, and eyes dewy with love.

"Framp! Framp, come here, you mutt!" A tall young man hove into view from the parking lot in back, a leash dangling from one hand.

"I hope Frampton hasn't drooled on you," he said as he mounted the steps to the porch. "He dotes on pretty girls, and I can't teach him to restrain himself."

"I—I like dogs," Alison said, patting the rough head of the fawning animal.

"Frampton, *heel,* darn it!"

The dog cast friendly eyes at his master but made no move to obey.

Alison had to laugh. She could see the young man's exasperated affection for his pet and the pet's amiable tolerance for him.

"Maybe if he had a more appropriate name..." she suggested mildly.

"He's named Frampton because of a remarkable likeness to an uncle of mine who carried the same moniker. The uncle was a nice old boy who had not more sense of propriety than this mutt. Oh, can you tell me if this place is the Honoria Nursing Home?"

"Yes, it is," Alison said.

"Are you a patient?"

"I am for a short while. Are you?"

"I'm Joe Lansing. I'm here for a supposed rest cure, and I hope all the patients look like you!"

"I haven't seen the other patients," Alison said. "I arrived here just a while ago."

"Well," Joe Lansing sighed, "I'd better go in and face whoever it is. May Frampton stay with you?"

Alison nodded and watched the tall young man enter the home. He was attractive and maybe he'd make her short stay here less boring. He had black hair, brown eyes, and looked to be in his late twenties, about six or seven years older than she. His face was lean, well sculpted, and bronzed by the sun. A less likely candidate for a rest cure would be hard to imagine!

Alison was getting restless, and it was becoming cold. She shivered in the chilly air.

Just as she was about to tie the dog to her chair and go inside, Joe erupted through the door.

"A doctor!" he raged. "That's what he calls himself! I can call myself a fruit tree, but don't expect me to grow peaches on my arms!"

"I won't," Alison said, holding back a laugh.

"He says I'm sicker than I thought I was. He says I'll have to stay here at least six weeks. He says he has to know my financial background and if I have any family."

"You're talking about Dr. Pitt, I guess. He's really all right. How did you find Honoria?"

"Entrancing! Just about as entrancing as a black widow spider."

Alison couldn't hold back her mirth any longer. It felt great to laugh. It had been a long time since her last laugh. This young man, this Joe, was going to do her good.

"There are only two good aspects about this incarceration," said Joe. "One is you and the other is that I can keep Frampton with me if I accept a very small room in the back. Shall we go in?"

Dr. Pitt met them. "Ah," he said, "I see you've met, and this is the nice little doggie." He reached out with one tentative finger to pat the dog's head. "I'll see you both tomorrow. Eat everything put before you now. It's important, remember. Particularly the beef broth. Good for your health."

"Yuck," Joe said as the doctor left the house.

Alison was herded away by the nurse, Nola. "You're to have dinner in your room, dear," the woman said. "If you're a good girl, maybe tomorrow you can join the others."

Alison wasn't averse to being by herself. She felt tired but no longer dispirited. She could thank Joe and the ridiculous dog for that.

That night she found she couldn't sleep in her big airy bedroom. There were too many unfamiliar noises—the sound of the sea, the wind breathing in heavy gusts, and the faint melancholy chime of a far-away buoy, the rattle of an ill-fitting window, and the old-age creaking of the house itself.

Then Alison heard a sound like a whimpering baby. At first it frightened and distressed her, but when she reasoned that the plaintive noise came from sea gulls, she had to smile at her alarm.

She fell asleep with the smile still on her pretty face.

Chapter Two

"I'll tell you," a plump, white-haired old woman bellowed, "he has the imagination of a tree stump." The loud voice stopped Alison in her tracks as she was entering the dining room.

"Just because he wears a white coat and rubber gloves and smells like a pickled toad," the old woman went on, "doesn't mean—hello! We have a new one with us! A pretty one, for a change! Come in, dear. Don't mind my ranting. I'm harmless."

Alison went up to the dining table.

"I'm Alison Munro," she said.

"*My* name is Lowell, Mrs. Lowell, and I just love your honey-blond hair and your

17

blue eyes. Only thing is, you're too skinny. You don't mind me being frank, do you?"

Alison took the seat held out for her by a weak-looking, pale young man.

"Thank you, ma'am," she said to the old woman. "But they do say that you can't be too rich or too thin."

The polite young man laughed in a strange, strangled way, as if laughter came hard to him.

"And thank *you,* sir," Alison added, smiling at him.

Honoria Stevens was sitting at the head of the oval table, coyly tossing her pink-red curls while giving little whinnies of mirth at an elderly gentleman's whispers.

Around the table were the loud-voiced old woman, the old man, the pale young man, Honoria, and Alison. There were also some empty seats.

Honoria's coy smile disappeared as she glanced at Alison.

"My dear," she said, "you are supposed to take your meals in your room until Doctor gives his permission to eat here. Didn't Rose, the maid, bring you your breakfast?"

"Oh, yes," Alison said cheerily, "but I sent it back. I don't like eating in a bedroom."

"I see," Honoria said. "We'll have to reach an understanding later on. In the meantime, you may have two boiled eggs, a piece of toast, and a cup of beef broth."

"I'd prefer coffee to broth," Alison said.

"I'm sure you would, my dear. Rose," she called to a thin little maid, "bring Miss Munro a cup of bouillon."

Alison turned to Honoria Stevens with the biggest, sunniest, most insincere smile she could muster.

"Mrs. Stevens, I'm afraid there'll be no understanding between us if you insist on my eating or drinking what you believe, in your no doubt honest and genuine opinion, to be in my best interests. I *won't* touch beef bouillon for breakfast and I *do* want coffee."

Alison really had no terrific yearning for coffee just now, but it was a matter of principle.

Honoria's mouth turned down as she stood up.

"Rose," she said, "bring Miss Munro a

cup of coffee. I shall have a talk with Doctor."

As she left the silent room, Joe Lansing came in.

"Is anybody else freezing to death?" he asked the breakfasters. "I can't close my windows and even my dog's feet are chattering."

The old woman looked extremely pleased. "Oh, bully!" she exclaimed. "We have *two!*"

She didn't need to explain. It was clear she meant there were two new ones at the home to complain about things.

Mrs. Lowell winked at Joe. "Son," she said, "it's supposed to be good for you, all this frigid fresh air. I've learned"—her voice dropped to a whisper—"how to close my windows and nobody knows the difference. I'll show you if you want."

Joe said, "Madam, you are a saint. Now what's for breakfast? Bouillon again? They must make it by the tankful!"

"Supposed to be good for you, too," Alison murmured.

"Subtle, that's very subtle," Joe said. "Only the very astute recognize the value of subtlety, the pleasure of being able to make fine distinctions. Do you know the Eskimos have a whole batch of different words for different types of snow?"

"What has that got to do with beef broth?" Alison asked.

"If you have to ask," Joe said with an air of superiority, "then I've been mistaken about your perspicacity. Too bad. Where's the coffee?"

It had to be explained to him that the broth was served in lieu of coffee. He protested but not too much.

The others at the table, although virtually finished with their meal, remained in their seats. The pale young man, Toby Weston, hooted a kind of laugh that he quickly engulfed in his napkin. The old man who had been making Honoria giggle, and whose name was Mr. Keene, cleared his throat and murmured something about a fresh breeze in this old house.

"Mrs. Lowell," Alison said to the old woman, "you were saying something when I came into the dining room, something about a doctor. Was it Dr. Pitt you were taking about?"

"I was. That man wouldn't know the

difference between a Sheraton desk and a hospital gurney."

"But not knowing things like that doesn't mean he's not a good general practitioner, does it?"

"Perhaps not. You may have a point there. Still, I hate to give him the benefit of the doubt. Well, off to the daily routine."

The old woman stood up and Alison was immediately reminded of a tea cozy. Mrs. Lowell was short and her plump figure was swathed in layers of padded material.

Joe politely helped her with her chair, then winked at Alison and left with his cup of bouillon in his hand.

Mr. Keene cleared his throat for the dozenth time. "Glad to have you with us, young lady. Just what is your complaint?"

"Complaint?"

"I mean your ailment. You must be sick or you wouldn't be here."

Alison carefully explained about her lung infection, minimizing it.

"Well, I hope you get better fast even if nothing serious is the matter with you. Have a good morning." He rose and left.

The pale young man, Toby, moved next to Alison, who was finishing her hard-won coffee.

"Uh," he said and stopped. Then he tried to smile, which seemed difficult for him. His mouth tilted to one side and opened like a trap.

"Uh," he repeated, "I'm allowed to take a short walk every day. Would—would you like to walk with me this morning?"

"That would be nice. What time?"

It was arranged that after the doctor's visit they would bundle up and walk along the cliff.

Dr. Pitt came early and was closeted with Honoria for quite a long time.

Alison obediently waited for him in her room. Rose, the waitress-chambermaid, had made her bed, tidied the room, and put out clean towels. Alison decided to pass the time with a book from a small shelf near the bed.

A pleasant mystery story was getting her full attention when the door opened and the nurse, Nola Brown, ushered in the doctor.

"Yesterday I asked that you knock before entering," Alison said. "I meant it."

"Alison, my dear," the doctor said in a playful voice, "we mustn't lose our sense of fairness, must we? Nola here has orders to enter the patients' rooms when it's necessary. Now be a reasonable girl!"

"I'm sorry that I don't conform, Doctor. Perhaps it's best that I leave this place."

"Now, now, let's not be hasty. I have a few things to discuss with you, my dear. I understand you have been making waves, refusing this and that and generally behaving in a childish fashion. But you must realize certain things. One, beef broth is a necessary part of our health program. Two, you have to—"

"Let's get this straight, Doctor. I want coffee for breakfast. I want people to knock before entering my room. Is that too much to ask?"

Alison's annoyance was growing. She could feel the heat of her flushed face and was aware of her pulse throbbing in her temples.

After he had examined her, the doctor sighed. "I don't like to make exceptions," he said. "But because I was fond of your father, I'll go along with your demands. However, you *must* drink your bouillon at least twice a day. Will you?"

"Yes."

"There's my pretty patient. Come, Nola, we have others to see."

They closed the door behind them as they left. Alison's hands were clenched, but she quickly relaxed. She had won this round. There would be others, but she would stand firm and face them when they came.

An hour later Alison saw from her window that the doctor had finished making his inspections and examinations. She bundled up and went downstairs.

Toby was waiting for her. He looked eager and bashful at the same time. He would be quite good-looking, Alison thought, if he weren't so pale, if he had any spark of animation at all, if he were a little bit more masculine.

They started walking at a good, brisk pace.

After a few minutes, Toby said, "Must we go so fast?"

"Oh." Alison looked remorseful. "I'm

sorry. I forgot you're a patient here. What—what is..."

She had trouble finishing her question.

Toby stood still and panted a bit. "I really don't know what's wrong with me," he said. "I came here to rest up after a bad bout of flu, about ten days ago. I'm over the flu, I think, but I'm so tired, so sleepy all the time. I suppose it's the sea air. At any rate, I sleep wonderfully well every night now, though I used to be an insomniac. I'm grateful for that."

Alison saw Frampton approaching at a full gallop. She felt Toby cringe as the big dog sprinted toward them.

"Don't be afraid," she said. "Frampton is a friendly animal—just overenthusiastic."

Frampton had skidded to a stop by that time and had taken Alison's hand in his mouth and held it gently while his adoring eyes gazed into hers.

"N-nice dog," Toby said nervously. "Does he belong to the new patient, Landers or something?"

"Lansing. Yes, Frampton is his and Joe has very little control over him. It's a good thing the mutt is so amiable."

At that moment they saw Joe Lansing heading toward them at a brisk trot. Frampton wagged his tail and then seemed torn in two. Would he stay with the pretty girl or go to his master? The master won out, and the big brown dog bounded away.

Soon Joe caught up to Alison and Toby. "You know," he said, "it's a moot question whether Framp loves me or pretty girls best."

"Love?" Toby said. "Would you call it love? And what is love, anyway."

"At the risk of sounding like a mushy greeting card," Joe said, "I believe in love!"

"So do I," Alison said.

"Well, maybe I do, too," Toby said. "Uh, I think I'll leave you two now. Pretty soon it'll be bouillon time and a short siesta before lunch. I'm not very strong, you see. I'm delicate, the doctor says. I must conserve my strength and energy."

When Toby left, Alison and Joe struck out at a fast pace, Frampton gamboling in front.

For a while they didn't talk, but then Joe slowed down. "I'm very sorry for that young man," he said.

"Toby Weston? Why?"

"Not only is he a hypochondriac, but he's full of self-pity. Self-pity is a most destructive emotion."

"Maybe he seems that way because he's so sleepy and tired all the time."

"Being tired and sleepy seems to be catching around here. Mrs. Lowell was going to bed as I left, and Mr. Keene was asleep in the chair in the front room. I understand there are four more patients, bed patients, and they probably only wake up for their beef broth. I wonder . . ."

"What?" Alison asked.

"Never mind. Just a thought. Tell me something about yourself, where your home is, why you're here, where you'll go when you leave."

"You first," she said.

"Okay. Obviously, when very young I was handsome and lovable and walked at six months and was doing algebra at nine months," Joe teased.

"And you've never recovered! Poor soul!"

"That wasn't the reaction I'd hoped for," he said. "It would have been nicer if you'd said something like 'You're still lovable.'"

"All right," said Alison, laughing. "You're handsome and lovable. You can still walk and no doubt you can do arithmetic."

"That's more like it!"

"You haven't said where you live, what sort of work you do, or anything about your family," Alison went on.

"I have no family, I do some research, and my present home is here. Now you."

"I have no family, either. My home is in Aiken, South Carolina, where I'll go when I leave here."

"Do they have a hospital there?" Joe asked.

"A very good one. Why?"

"Just curious. Shall we walk further or start back now?"

"Let's get back in time for our beef broth," Alsion said.

When they returned to the nursing home, Honoria stood waiting for them at the door. She greeted them with a smile that was deceptively open and sweet.

"You'll have to time yourselves a little better," she said pleasantly. "You almost missed your eleven o'clock nourishment.

Cups of broth are in each of your rooms. Drink it all up and have a snooze before lunch."

Up in her room, Alison took a sip. It didn't quite taste the way bouillon should. Or so she thought. Once again the contents of the cup went down the drain.

Chapter Three

It was after lunch and everybody was supposed to be having another siesta. Alison was reading her mystery novel and occasionally looking out the window at the rough ocean and the sea gulls that crossed the gray sky above.

A knock on her door was welcome. She was tired of enforced rest periods.

It was Joe.

"Alison, may I borrow your car? Mine won't start."

"Of course, you may. Where are you going?"

"Going to the nearest city. I'll be back before dinner."

Alison almost asked to go with him but decided against it. She was here to be cured of the small spot on her lung and to get rested. She got her keys from her purse.

"You may need gas," she said. "I think there's only a quarter tank left."

"You're a dear. Thanks. See you later, honey."

If someone else had used an endearing term on such short acquaintance, Alison would have been annoyed. Yet she didn't mind when Joe did it. She rather liked it. But though she looked forward to seeing him again, she was surprised when he returned in less than ten minutes.

"Yours won't start either!" he said. "I looked under the hoods of both our cars. You know what? The distributor heads are gone!"

"You mean that someone—I can't believe this!"

"I mean someone has taken them. I mean we're isolated here. If they think that will stop me, they're mistaken." He started out the door, then turned.

"There's a telephone in Mrs. Stevens's

office, isn't there? I'll call a garage in Fairview. *And,*" he added, a threat in his voice, "I'll find out who the thief is if it's the last thing I do!"

"Could it be a type of prank?" Alison asked.

"That kind of humor leaves me cold." Joe stormed out and Alison could hear him pounding down the stairs.

In a minute she heard Honoria scolding him about his noise and his lack of consideration for resting patients. Then there was silence. Alison imagined Joe inside Honoria's pink, frilly room telephoning. How annoying to have a necessary part taken from your car! No wonder Joe was mad.

Why was he going to town, though? Wasn't he, like all the others, supposed to be taking a rest cure? You don't rest if you're gallivanting around the countryside. Oh, well, it was his own business.

She returned to her book. A walk again this afternoon would be nice while the weather held—it was supposed to worsen tomorrow.

There was another knock on Alison's

door. Joe barged in when she opened it. He was frowning savagely.

"I'll throttle that woman," he snarled.

"What's the trouble now?" Alison asked.

"The telephone is on the blink, so she says, and she won't let me use the nursing home's station wagon! She said the distributor heads had been removed on purpose because no one is allowed to leave until they have the doctor's okay. She actually said to me that *I* and another patient, meaning *you*, were troublemakers! Imagine!"

"Calm yourself, Joe. I understand your anger. Frustration has a way of creeping up on a person at a time like this, but you're not doing yourself any good by getting mad, you know. Rest cures aren't just for the body. The mind . . ." She hesitated. "Well, you might be paranoid."

"Oh, really! You know what I admire about you? You can't see a belt without hitting below it!"

"That's the nastiest thing anybody has ever said to me," Alison told him in an icy tone. "Now go away!"

"Oh, Alison! Forgive me! I'm a fool. My temper has been sorely tried this day.

Please don't be mad! Count on me, my dearest girl, for the last drop of blood from my body!"

Alison had to laugh at him. He was as ridiculous as his dog.

"Alison, I wasn't going to speak until I had proof. That's why I wanted to get to a pharmacy or lab or something. But so you won't stay angry with me, I'll tell you my suspicion. You know that sometimes nursing homes keep their patients tranquilized, don't you?"

Alison nodded while he walked toward the window. "I think it's a brutal thing to do, Joe. It keeps the poor old souls in such a zombielike state, they never recover. Are you saying—"

"The beef broth. I have a sample I was taking with me to be analyzed. But I didn't quite make it." He shrugged helplessly.

As Joe stared outside, Alison saw his jaw tighten. She ran to the window and watched Honoria enter the home's station wagon, then drive away.

"I guess I can revise my original plans," Joe said. "I'll just walk to Fairview, rent a car there, and—"

"You haven't got time for all that this

afternoon, Joe. Wait till tomorrow. I'll walk with you if I can. In the meantime, should we talk to or tell the others of your suspicion? I haven't swallowed any of the bouillon, have you?"

"A bit, maybe half a cup, and I had to fight off fatigue for a while afterward. I don't know about telling the others. They probably wouldn't believe it unless I had proof, and it's possible that some of them welcome the peace the broth gives them. Anyway, Alison, honey, we'll wait. I'm forgiven now, aren't I?"

"I guess so. Anyone, even a simpleminded soul like me, can change what she euphemistically calls her mind, can't she?"

"Big words. They prove you've got an extra sharp mind, my girl. And I'm counting on that mind to help me when I get proof of the violation of the patients' rights."

Alison had a worried frown marring her pretty face.

"It just occurred to me," she said slowly, "that maybe my father didn't have to die! Maybe he was sedated to death! Oh, no!" Her voice was filled with anguish. "Oh, no, it can't be possible!" She looked at Joe with pleading, tear-filled eyes. "It's not possible, is it? Tell me it isn't, Joe. Tell me!"

Joe took Alison in his arms. He kissed the top of her head, then her cheek, and finally his mouth found hers.

The door opened suddenly. Nola had a cup of broth in her hand. Seeing Alison in Joe's embrace, the nurse came close to spilling it.

"This is not allowed," she said sternly. "I'm afraid I'll have to report such shocking behavior. Will you please *leave,* Mr. Lansing."

"No, Joe," Alison said, wiping away her tears. "You may stay if you wish. I want you as witness to this nurse's breaking into my room without knocking. This is the third time and I won't put up with it!"

"Drink your bouillon," Nola said sharply. "When Mrs. Stevens comes back—when the doctor . . ." Her voice faded as she left, slamming the door behind her.

"She's as bad as Honoria," Joe said. "I suppose, though, she has her orders and we shouldn't be hard on her."

"Pollyanna," Alison grumbled. "That's *you!*"

"Sweetness and light. That's you. Let's go down to the front room and see if any other inmates are around. We might feel them out a little. What are you doing with your broth?"

"It goes down the drain the way the others have," Alison said.

The front room was comfortable. Easy chairs faced an unlit fireplace. The mantelpiece had two blue Chinese dogs and a snuffbox. The floor was so thickly carpeted, it almost felt like a cloud. Alison believed it was to cushion a fall made by an unsteady patient. Well, she couldn't complain about that.

They had the room to themselves.

"Sit down, darling," Joe said. "I want you to tell me all you can about Dr. Pitt, and then I want you to tell me about your father's illness. Try not to get too upset. It's important that I know."

"I'm sure I don't know why it's important, but I'll try. We have a summer cottage in Fairview. Once or twice in the last couple of years, one of us, with a cold or a sprain or something, went to Dr. Pitt. The old doctor that was here before Pitt was a dear. We liked him much better than—well, anyway, in August I went home to Aiken to attend a friend's wedding. While I was there, I received a wire saying Daddy was ill. I flew back here and found him in this nursing home. Dr. Pitt said he was suffering from food poisoning. The change in Daddy was frightening. He'd been so healthy, I thought, and tanned and full of pep. But now in the nursing home, he was positively unrecognizable."

Alison was taut with the strain of talking about her late father. She paused a moment.

"Yes, darling, go on," Joe said. He held her hand lightly and squeezed it.

"He was..." Alison held back a sob that caught in her throat. "He was dead in a few days." Her lower lip trembled a little until she caught it firmly in her teeth.

"What was the medical report?" Joe asked.

"Food poison. Botulism. I—I took his body back to Aiken where Mother is buried. Then I came back to Fairview to close the cottage, maybe sell it, and I caught a beast of a cold. Dr. Luther Pitt was kind and sent me here to the nursing home."

"That's all?"

"Yes. Except I heard him say to Honoria that she couldn't have known Daddy's estate was tied up in a trust fund for me. Not that that's important."

"It could well be. Oh, here's Mrs. Lowell! How are you, Mrs. Lowell? You're looking great."

Mrs. Lowell wasn't looking great at all, Alison thought. She still was as round as a tea cozy, but her face was drawn and pale. Her bedroom slippers were loose on her bony white feet.

"I slept so hard," Mrs. Lowell said, "I don't know which side is up."

"Sit here," Joe said. "And here comes Mr. Keene and Toby Weston. It's like a tea party! But," he added, "I suppose instead of tea we'll have beef broth!"

There was a spate of polite laughter, and Mr. Keene, despite his languid look, said, "It's better than nothing, I always say."

Toby Weston was like a zombie, Alison thought. Poor Toby with his slow-moving body, his hesitant manner, his watery eyes. But even with his apparent weakness, he looked sort of hopeful with his earnest, heart-piercing smile. She smiled back at him.

There was a silence while three people tried to recover from their inertia. The other two, Alison and Joe, looked at each other knowingly. Then Alison turned away, feeling sad and disturbed.

Joe interrupted the quiet. "Has anyone looked at the sky lately? Layers of clouds are blanketing the horizon, growing thicker, and the sun has a wintry glower."

"How poetic!" Mrs. Lowell said.

"Thank you. Which reminds me, is anyone here the owner of a car I could borrow? Toby?"

"No, I don't own a car."

"Mr. Keene, have you a—"

"My car is in storage in Portland."

"I don't suppose you, Mrs. Lowell—"

"No, young man. My car and my chauffeur are in New York waiting for me to summon them."

"Well, I thought I'd try," Joe sighed.

Alison felt that another silence was about to ensue.

"Toby, tell us about your family," she said. "Do you have any brothers? Or sisters?"

"I have no family at all," Toby said abruptly.

"Oh, neither have I," Alison said. "Mrs. Lowell, do you have children or—"

"I'm the only one left in my family," she answered sadly.

Well, that was a jolly start, Alison thought wryly. What else can you do to cheer things up, you dummy?

Mr. Keene came to life. "All of us are in blessed singleness, aren't we? Unless *you*, young man ..." He pointed to Joe.

"Oh, I'm without a family, too. I wonder if the bed patients are also unmarried and childless. Anybody know?"

"Yes," Mrs. Lowell said. "The four bed patients were up and about when I first got here. Poor souls, they have declined in a hurry. I believe they're all single people with no one worrying about them. I at least have a staff of servants who get salaries while I'm alive."

"Who started this gloomy talk?" Joe asked.

"I guess I did," Alison said. "Sorry."

"Oh, it doesn't matter for some," Toby said. "Some have minds that atrophied years ago."

Honoria bustled in. "You have a treat in store for you, dear ones! Doctor will have dinner with us! Isn't that lovely?"

They all made polite if not joyful responses and, when the portly doctor entered the front room, Honoria almost collapsed in a fit of obsequiousness: "Have this chair.... Are you quite comfortable? May I get you anything?"

The afternoon was too gray and cold for walks. Alison and Joe played "fetch" with Frampton and a ball from the porch, and finally it was time for dinner.

Before long everyone was seated at the dining-room table. Alison watched the doctor as each bite disappeared quickly between his full red lips. Occasionally, between swallows, those lips issued words of amiable response to any questions put to him. Her appetite failed.

Late that night Alison heard the cries again. How could sea gulls sound like a human calling, "Please! Oh, please! Help!"?

But did she really hear that, or was she imagining it?

Chapter Four

"We have a very aggrieved nurse on our hands," Honoria said to Alison the next morning after most of the others had left the breakfast table. "You have insulted her, you know. She is truly a good person, Alison."

"A truly good person can be insufferable," Alison replied. "I don't think a decent, intelligent person needs to barge into my room the way she does. A simple knock on my door will get a response without irritating me. Surely that's not too much to ask. Whatever happened to that sweet nurse you used to have, Gertrude Smith? I loved her."

"We don't speak of Gertrude Smith," Honoria said sharply. In a rather strange way, she was looking out of the corner of her steely eyes without turning her head. Was it to quickly veil the alarm that had leapt into her countenance? Was there a secret there?

"*I* speak of Gertrude Smith," Alison said stoutly. "I liked her and I ask *again* whatever happened to her?"

"She left us, that's all. Now, Miss Munro, Alison dear, you really mustn't make any more trouble. We have a hard enough time with only one nurse, one maid, one cook, and a handyman. We do the best we can."

Honoria had put a pathetic note into her voice, which did not fool Alison one bit.

"You may be assured that I won't make trouble if I, in turn, am not annoyed by Nola." Alison nodded a goodby and left.

Toby was waiting for her.

"I'm feeling better this morning," he said with the awful egoism of an ailing person.

"I'm glad to hear that," Alison said. "I'm going out on the porch to watch the storm come. Want to join me?"

"Oh—oh, no, I don't like storms. They're dangerous." He thanked her with the quick grimace that was his smile.

"Okay then, see you later." Alison didn't show that she considered poor Toby spineless. He was a sad example of a self-pitying rabbit, she thought with compassion.

She wrapped herself up well and went onto the porch, drinking in the fresh, crisp air.

When a storm is on its way, she thought, it does something to the basic part of one—to that deep, dark place where all reasoning is based on instinct.

She sniffed the ozone-spiced air and re-velled in the electric energy she felt coursing through her whole being.

Suddenly the storm was upon her, wild wind, slashing rain, thunder, lightning, and billowing black clouds. It was magnificent.

"Bravo!" she cried as noise piled on noise and more thunder crashed.

Where were the sea gulls now? Did they hide from the turbulence? That one with the crying, almost human voice—again she'd decided it was a sea gull—was he still around? Would he disturb her again tonight? A thought went skittering across her mind so fast she didn't catch it. She tried to make her mind a blank so, if it reappeared, she could grab it. What was it? Why was it distressing, this vanished impression? The storm no longer held her interest, and she went inside and up to her room.

Alison was deep in her mystery novel when all at once her eyes flared open.

She had it, she'd caught it, that skittering thought that had tried to elude her. It was those cries in the night, the almost familiar tone of the appeal for help, the voice not of a sea gull but of a woman she'd known. Who? Where?

Was her imagination playing tricks on her, after all? Had the atmosphere of this nursing home begun to addle her brain? Or what? She felt herself tensing up. She could now feel a definite menace and evil. A tumbling knot of fear was in the pit of her stomach.

When a knock sounded on her door, Alison rushed to open it and literally fell into Joe's arms.

"What a nice welcome," he started to say, then saw Alison's distress. "Darling, what's the matter?"

"Oh, Joe, I'm all upset. I just feel that there's something very wrong with this place, something frightening."

"Of course there is, love. We already suspect it, don't we?"

"I mean something beyond the sedation of the patients. Oh, I don't know *what* I mean."

"There, there, sweetheart. You're trembling. Buck up! Don't lose your nerve!"

Alison gave a smothered chortle. "I haven't any nerve left to lose!"

"Good, you haven't lost your sense of humor, anyway. I had a little talk with Honoria a few minutes ago. This will pep you up, darling. She told me that *you* have an adder's tongue and I told her that I 'like to think so, dear!' Then she drew herself up and wished she could see her way to a more charitable attitude, and I told her that if she saw herself as the soul of charity, that was her business. But she was mistaken."

Joe, as he related this, had a wicked

twinkle in his eye and Alison had to smile at him. She immediately felt better.

"I guess I'm just hysterical, Joe. Bear with me, will you, when I tell you . . ." She hesitated.

"Yes, darling? You started to say . . ."

"At night I hear someone calling for help. The first night I thought it was a sea gull, but now I think something else."

"Now you believe it's someone in distress. Any idea who?"

"Of course not. Is it my imbecilic imagination, Joe? Am I losing my marbles?"

Joe took her into his arms. "Don't even *dream* of such a thing, love. There has to be an explanation. Now, relax. I want to ask you some questions, but I think we should go downstairs. It's almost beef-broth time. And if we're caught in your room again, there'll be a scandal. Come along."

They found the front room deserted, and Joe told Alison to sit close beside him so he could whisper his questions.

"You told me, darling, that when you came back here, your father was almost unrecognizable. Didn't you?"

She could only nod her head and try to stop the lump in her throat from choking her. "I'm—I'm sorry I go to pieces each time Daddy is mentioned. I should have more control. Go on."

"How changed was he, Alison? Take your time, cry if you want."

His words steadied her. "He was terribly thin. Even his hair had thinned and was grayer. His eyes, when they saw me, were dull and expressionless. If you want the truth, I knew it was Daddy just because he was wearing his college ring and had on a pair of pajamas I had given him."

"Did he smile? Could you see his teeth?"

"He made a sort of wry face at me, but that was all. No—once he mentioned horseback riding and talked about the expense of the nursing home. But his words were mushy, and I wasn't sure I heard right. Why are you asking these things?"

"Just interested. Alison, try not to rock the boat. You need to keep the staff here on your side."

"That'll be hard to do, Joe."

"I know. Just be careful." He left her abruptly without a kiss or a handshake

or a friendly wink, and Alison had a sink-
ing feeling.

Her breath seemed trapped in a hot little pocket at the base of her throat. She
remembered a few other things pertain-
ing to her father that she might have told
Joe. For instance, the nice nurse,
Gertrude, who seemed upset about all her
patients, had seemed especially concerned about her father. And it was odd
how her father seemed to enjoy the beef
broth when he'd always disliked thin
soups.

But where had Joe disappeared to? It
was rainy and not a good day for a walk.
Surely he wasn't walking to town to rent
a car so he could have the beef broth analyzed, was he?

Alison went up to her room, reaching
her door just as Nola Brown was approaching with her cup of broth. The girl
took the bouillon from the silent, pouting
nurse, entered her room, and poured it
down the drain. She hoped the plumbing
didn't object.

She tried to go back to her book, but
her mind kept turning to Joe and his
questions.

The minutes dragged by with sadistic slowness. Perhaps the company of the others would be preferable to her solitary waiting, waiting. Waiting for what? She decided to leave her room.

Toby was downstairs in the front room, slowly sipping his "nourishment." He looked at her with his large, watery brown eyes. "Did—did the storm scare you inside?" he asked.

"No. I loved it. I'm afraid it's about over," Alison answered.

And now she saw that Honoria was curled up in a pose too kittenish for the tall woman. Honoria was listening to Mr. Keene, whose paunch rested on his lap and whose mouth kept flapping in a whispered conversation.

The secret of victory is to attack. Alison suddenly remembered that bit of advice from her father.

"Oh, Honoria," she called in her sweetest voice, "I wasn't bothered by Nola today. You know why? It was because I relieved her of the bouillon *outside* my room."

A faint flush appeared on Honoria's cheeks. "You are the soul of consideration," she said smoothly. "As always."

Toby sent Alison a glance that slid over her like quicksilver. It was a frightened glance, but it showed all the symptoms of a beginning love.

No, Alison thought. This can't be allowed to burgeon. This must be nipped in the bud.

Honoria uncurled herself. She lowered her voice and there was a thin layer of oil in her tone.

"Alison dear, you've been here two nights and already you're quite certain you could run this home better than I, aren't you? Well, I'd like to see you try."

"So would I," Alison said. "There are a few things I'd like to change."

"Now, now," Mr. Keene said. "Some of us have forgotten we are here for *rest* and *no worry* and serene, happy outlooks. Now can't we simply relax without fussing?"

"You are right, Mr. Keene," Alison said. "I'm sorry if I upset anyone. I'm afraid I'm too impulsive."

A thin smile that looked as if it had been etched with a razor touched Honoria's face.

"Impulse excuses a myriad of faults," she murmured.

Alison remembered that Joe had warned her not to rock the boat. He wanted her to be liked by the staff and that included Honoria.

"Yes, I'm truly sorry if I've made anyone uneasy or unhappy. I'll try to be more considerate."

An important step on the road to success, Alison told herself, is learning to tell a good lie and stick with it. She smiled at everyone.

Honoria's eyes had a hard, flickering light in them, and Alison felt the pricklings of foreboding pull at her skin. She had made an enemy of the woman, and no matter how she tried to win her over, she knew it would be futile.

So be it, Alison said to herself. Let's just coast.

Toby spoke up. "You haven't made *me* uneasy or unhappy," he said rather fiercely. "I think you're tops!"

"Why, thank you, Toby! What a nice thing to say!"

"Would you like to go for a walk?" Toby

asked then. "It's not raining now."

"I'd love to."

If Alison would have preferred to walk with Joe, she didn't reveal this wish. Besides, Joe had seemingly vanished like a puff of smoke.

Toby and Alison wore coats and mufflers, gloves and head coverings, but still the chill was penetrating.

"Is Maine always as cold as this in September?" Toby asked.

"Not usually, I think. But I'm never here in the fall, so I don't really know. I normally teach school in South Carolina in September."

The ocean was leaden gray and its waves were roiling and alarmingly tall. The smell of seaweed, a stimulating briny odor, filled the air. The sea cliffs glistened with salt spray, and sea gulls swooped, their graceful wings flapping, their yellow beaks cruelly hooked.

"I'm not the wimp you think I am," Toby suddenly said.

"Why, Toby, I never thought any such thing."

"Of course, you did. You were supposed

to, and so was everyone else. But I want
you to know that I'm not what I seem."

"I'm confused," Alison said. "Can you
explain?"

"Not for a while. Now that Joseph
Landers has gone—"

"Lansing."

"Okay, Lansing. Now that he's left,
maybe I'll have a chance with you."

"He hasn't left," Alison said. "He's out
for a while."

"Oh, no, he's gone. The clothes in his
room are gone and his dog is gone. Lansing has left for good, I'm sure. And all I
can say is, just because a snake sheds its
skin doesn't mean it quits being a snake."

Chapter Five

At first Alison was convinced that Toby had been mistaken when he'd said Joe had left. But when she went to Joe's room and found it open and bare of all his gear, she felt a dreadful emptiness. How could he have left for good without a real goodby? If he had gone just to have a sample of the beef broth tested, he would not have taken all of his things with him. She ran to the window to look for his car. It was still there and so was hers. Did that mean Joe had walked away, carrying all his belongings?

Her mind went back to her stroll with

Toby. It had been full of surprises. The
most distressing was his averred conviction that Joe had left for good. The most
surprising was that when she'd slipped on
a slick portion of the cliff, Toby had
grabbed her with astonishing strength.
And she had seen a light in his brown
eyes that astounded her with its tough-
ness.

But Toby was a frail, uninteresting hypochondriac. How could he, all of a sudden, display a manly force and a complete
change of character? She found herself
viewing him in a new light. He was certainly good-looking. She had always
known that. It had been his soppy self-
interest that had turned her off.

His brown eyes no longer seemed watery or pleading. They had originally reminded Alison of a trapped, frightened
animal, and he had seemed to be in a zombie state most of the time. She now at-
tributed this state to the beef broth. That
was, if Joe's suspicions were correct.

"Toby, you told me that until you came
here you were an insomniac. But now you
sleep a lot."

"Lies, all lies! I always slept well. And

I've never had a sick day in my life."

"Why are you here, then?" Alison had asked.

"Poking around."

"I suppose you don't want me to ask the inevitable question, so I won't," she said. "You'll tell me if you want to. Now what I want to know is, do you drink the bouillon that's so often served us?"

"I do when I'm being watched. I pretend to enjoy it, but you'll find that I don't take more than a sip or two. Do you have a hunch about it?"

"Yes, and so does Joe. I believe that Joe has gone to have our 'nourishment' analyzed. He was planning to take a sample—but why would he pack up everything and leave as if he weren't coming back? Of course, his car must still be here. That's because our dear Honoria had the handyman remove the distributor heads from both his car and mine. Is it true you don't own a car? I didn't know any young man could live without transportation."

"No, it's not true. I have one parked in Fairview."

"You're living a total lie here at Honoria Nursing Home, aren't you?" She had absently picked up an attractive piece of driftwood and was surprised by its heaviness. It would make a nice decoration for some living room.

"I am." His face had tightened with anger, but Alison could tell he was not mad at her. "And I'm trusting you not to betray me. When I'm back at the home, I'll be the wimp they all expect. Now, Alison, I've told you a lot about me, so please tell me more about you."

She said, "You've told me just enough to inflame my curiosity, Toby, but I promise not to reveal your secret personality. Or rather, your true personality. As for me, no secrets at all. I live in Aiken, South Carolina, where I'm a fourth-grade teacher. But I already told you most of that."

"I think we'd better go back now. I'm greatly tempted to tell you why and how I'm a patient here, but I mustn't yet. Let's go."

"I must say, Toby, you've given me an even better mystery than the book I'm reading. May I try to solve it?"

"You can try, but you haven't any clues, and I'm not about to give you one. There's danger lurking around us. Take my word for it. Now I'm going to change to Caspar Milquetoast again."

He did. He was a wonderful actor. His whole body, his face, his manner—they all became apologetic, shy, and rather pathetic. It was quite mind-boggling, Alison thought. She looked at him with admiration, but at a slight shake of his head, she was reminded to treat him like the sad sack she'd thought he was.

Back at the nursing home Alison whiled away the hours by reading, speculating about Toby's disclosure, worrying about Joe, and throwing beef broth down the drain. If one was really sick, she thought, it wouldn't be so boring here. If there was something constructive she could do, the time would fly. But what was there for her? Maybe Joe had taken a sample of broth to be analyzed. But even if it contained some sedative, no crime was probably involved. Doubtless many nursing homes and such tranquilized their patients. It was a bad practice, Alison thought, but that didn't mean it was illegal.

Suddenly she couldn't stand her room another minute. She decided she would quietly visit the bed patients. She'd talk to them if they were awake, tiptoe away if they were asleep.

The first room Alison went to was occupied by a gray-haired woman. Alison listened to the slow, drugged breathing and withdrew.

The next room housed an elderly man whose bleary eyes focused on her and held an instant of alertness, then faded.

"Hello," Alison said, coming farther into the room. "Can I do anything for you?"

"Oh, nothing, nothing!" he croaked. "I've just had all my worries taken from me!" His eyes had brightened again.

"How wonderful!" Alison said. "It's lovely not to worry, isn't it? What's your name, sir?"

"Yes, you see, I'll be allowed to stay here the rest of my life. I'll be taken care of. All I had to do was to sign a few papers and that's all. I'm so relieved! No more worries about money or anything. Are you a new nurse? Oh, yes, my name is Frank Newman."

"No, I'm a patient, too, Mr. Newman. I'm so glad you're happy and I'll come visit you again."

Alison left the old man muttering to himself, chortling now and then as if he'd put something over on someone.

The next bed patient was napping peacefully, and the fourth was snoring like a chain saw.

Alison returned to her room. She opened the ocean-side window and drank in the spicy scents. It was good to get rid of the smell of sickness. The air was full of the sea, the pounding, vital sea. She loved it.

The second bed patient, Frank Newman, monopolized her thoughts. His happiness, his relief—they bothered her. His newfound joy was the product of a distorted, twisted, drug-clouded brain! Honoria and the doctor were taking advantage of him. What had he signed?

These musings gave Alison a queasy feeling in the pit of her stomach. And yet she must not fly off the handle without solid proof. Maybe there was no reason to be alarmed about the old man. Maybe he had signed a sort of lease that would keep him in the home forever. Was it wrong— if that was what he wanted? And that did seem to be what was making him happy.

Oh, how Alison wished Joe were here so she could talk it out with him! What about Toby? Could she discuss it with him? No, better not.

The evening meal was tasty, but it would have been more so if Joe were there. Mrs. Lowell talked about Dr. Pitt, whom she obviously held in low esteem.

"I irritate him," she guffawed. "And he conceals it poorly."

Honoria's smile was frozen on her face. Alison could almost feel sorry for the proprietor of the home.

Honoria so obviously venerated the doctor. "I believe," she said to Mrs. Lowell, "that I pointed out to you how splendid Doctor is! I told you not to annoy him, Mrs. Lowell. You deserve his reproaches."

"If there's one thing I can't stand," Mrs. Lowell said, "it's an 'I told you so' attitude."

There was the usual small talk among the patients, Toby making a few inane remarks, which Alison now knew were part of his masquerade. She did wonder *why* he was making himself sound like such a spiritless creature, but she felt he'd tell her eventually.

That night the remembrance of the eerie cries kept her tense. Alison lay rigid on her bed and listened to the wind buffeting the house; she heard the ocean, far below, pounding on the rocks. She quivered with a fear of the unknown, and her heart thudded sickeningly. Her eyes were wide open, but she lay still, unmoving, waiting, listening, every sense on edge.

And then the first cry came. It was a voice choked with tears, with frustration.

Alison shuddered. She was positive the cry was human. No sea gull could put such a tragic tone into its cries. Where could the sounds be coming from? And why did they come only at night? She answered the last question first. If it were an imprisoned patient, then she might be tranquilized during the day when the others were up and about—but allowed to be free of sedation when the others were asleep.

Oh, Joe! Joe! I need you, Alison thought. I need your advice, I need your support, I need your kisses!

She got up and went to the windows— first to the ocean-side one and then to the other. The cries were *not* coming from the outside! Where then? Alison prowled around her room and then around her bathroom.

The cries for help had stopped, but she had an idea. There was a large heat vent in the bathroom. Could that act like a sort of megaphone for someplace in the cellar?

Oh, please cry just one more time, she prayed to the distressed soul somewhere in the house. But there was only silence.

Thoroughly awake and terribly intrigued, Alison put on slacks, a sweater, and a pair of sneakers, formulating a plan in her mind. Perhaps her scheme was foolish, maybe even dangerous, but she'd always been impulsive.

She needed a weapon of some sort. What could she use if she were attacked? Attacked? Her stupid imagination was cast-

ing her as a heroine in a melodrama, she
told herself. However, she might make do
with the pretty piece of driftwood she'd
picked up earlier on her walk with Toby.

Alison's heart was like a trip-hammer
as she left her room. There were night-
lights on in the hall, but Alison kept to
the shadows as she crept down the stairs
and went to the rear of the house where
the kitchen was and where the cook, maid,
and handyman had their rooms. It was
also where Joe and his dog had had their
quarters. And suddenly Alison's concern
for the young man tore her apart.

She was like a tightly wound clock as
she found a door to the cellar and flipped
on the dim and dusty light bulb by the
stairway.

A sour, dank smell arose from below
and Alison almost turned back. But, no,
she told herself. She'd gotten this far and
it would be cowardly to give up. She
wished she had a flashlight. The shadows
were indigo pools and the one dim bulb
only exposed some cobwebs draping the
pipes.

It was even darker when Alison reached

the bottom. She could see the ghostly shape of a furnace, and beside it stood a large water heater. Beyond those two pieces of equipment, the cellar became a black pit of the unknown.

It was into this obscure area that she must venture. Alison was searching for the source of the desperate cry and it seemed to her she might locate it in this most forbidding, ominous place.

A sound like a sigh echoed through the cavernous cellar.

"Is—is someone there?" Alison called softly in a far-from-steady voice, holding up her piece of driftwood like a club.

The sigh came again, nearer this time. It wasn't a sorrowful sigh. It seemed almost threatening, if a sigh could be so termed.

Alison's stomach had drawn into a tight fist, and she could hardly breathe. What was she doing in this horrible, musty cellar? Why didn't she turn and flee back to the safety of her room? Why? Because maybe somebody needed her. Maybe somebody was locked up somewhere in the cellar?

Alison was determined to find the captive if there really was one. Wouldn't she be mortified if she found the cry was coming from a squeaky door blown about by the wind! Yet she knew with certainty that it hadn't been a door she'd heard.

No more tiptoeing or whispering in the dark, she told herself. No more stealth. She would talk to the hidden captive in a loud voice.

"Who is there?" Alison called. "Where is the woman who cries at night? Come on, where are you? Where are—"

Alison suddenly entered the deep darkness of unconsciousness as her head connected with something hard.

A while later she woke up with a sneeze from the dust all around her. She was lying flat on the filthy floor and her head seemed about to explode. Gingerly she turned over and sat up. She had a woozy feeling, but gradually the cellar stopped spinning around her. She examined herself for any broken bones or gashes and found none. Had she, in her wild burst of bravery, run into a beam that had knocked her out? She was sure she hadn't. Someone had hit her!

And where was her enemy? It was still

as dark as before and the only light came from the stairs, which seemed miles away.

She staggered to her feet and yelped as she was grabbed from behind. She had never known such terror before.

"Be quiet, Alison," her assailant hissed. "Go back to your room now and you won't be hurt."

"Who are you?" Alison croaked.

In the murky shadows—and in her excited frame of mind—his face seemed distorted, his eyes too closely set. He didn't look like anybody she knew, but his strength was monumental.

Chapter Six

Nothing would induce Alison to leave the security of her room again that night. A thousand cries for help would be ignored. She shivered as she lay there on her bed, asking herself many questions.

Just what had happened in the cellar? Who had attacked her, then let her go? Did she know him as he seemed to know her, and what was he doing in the cellar? Was he also looking for a woman who cried out in the night? Or was he merely following Alison?

The voice in the cellar—whose was it? Now that she thought about it, she real-

ized there had been something familiar
about it.

Alison struggled to control the shivers
of fear that persisted. She told herself she
was safe now. That was a lie, but she
couldn't run off alone in the dark. She told
herself to go to bed. She had to stay here
and find out what was really happening.
She told herself to stop yearning for Joe.

"Nuts to him," she said to an empty
wastebasket. "Who needs him?"

I do, her mind said. I need Joe desperately. I need him *now!*

Don't rock the boat, he'd warned her,
but she'd kept on rocking it, maybe en-
dangering her very life.

She finally managed to catch some sleep
and thankfully woke up to a sunny day.
Alison planned to walk a long way—to
walk away the terrors of the night before.
Her head hurt just behind her ear, and
there was a tender knot that protested
when she touched it. But her pain made
her all the more determined to clear up
whatever was going on here.

Breakfast was being served when she
appeared in the dining room. She wore a

yellow sweater over gray slacks and had tied her blond hair back with a yellow bow. She looked more cheerful than she felt.

The breakfasters seemed particularly subdued this morning. Their voices were low and Honoria was not present.

"Poor old man," Mrs. Lowell whispered. "And he seemed so much better last week."

"Why, he was laughing to himself when I passed his room yesterday," Mr. Keene said.

"Who are you talking about?" Alison asked.

"Frank Newman," Mrs. Lowell answered.

"Is he worse?" Alison questioned.

"He's dead," Mr. Keene said. "Died last night or early this morning."

The shock of the news made a chill run down Alison's spine. "Oh, how sad! I talked to him in the afternoon and he was so happy about his secure future. He—"

She stopped as a dreadful suspicion rushed into her mind. Oh, surely not! She must not think such things! But it was so pat! He signed something and then he was dead! She swallowed a lump in her throat.

Voices, loud voices, echoed down the staircase.

"Where is it? If you've lost it, you fool, you'll be very, *very* sorry!" That was Honoria's voice.

"I haven't seen it, really I haven't. Maybe someone else picked it up." That was Nola's voice in response. "Maybe Rose or even Nancy could have taken it away."

"Stop making excuses! Find it!"

The breakfasters had stopped eating and were listening avidly.

When Honoria stormed into the dining room, all heads turned toward her. Her eyes were like ice chips frozen from murky water. Her whole body was vibrating with anger, and her face was bathed in white fury. Her struggle for composure was evident. She forced her voice to be quiet, but everybody could hear crackles of lightning in it.

"Did anyone here remove Mr. Newman's bouillon cup from his room? Either last night or this morning? It's quite important that I find it. Please, I'd just like to know if anyone has seen it." She smiled her broad, metallic smile. "I mean, I won't blame anyone or anything like that."

Alison's eyes flicked over to Toby. At that moment he looked neither submissive nor colorless. There was more jaw than she'd noticed before and his clenched fists were quite powerful. He was no longer a mouse sandwich for a tomcat. He was there to be reckoned with, but as she stared at him, he got himself back into character with a wimpy expression and eyes that had been dead for a thousand years.

"What's so important about a bouillon cup?" Mrs. Lowell asked. "To my knowledge, all your china is dime-store quality. What a fuss about nothing! Aha! Here comes Miss Thermometer herself. Maybe she has the missing treasure."

Nola gave Mrs. Lowell a venomous glance, then turned to Honoria. "It's gone. I've questioned Nancy and Rose and Sam. None of them have been near Mr. Newman's room. So they say. *I* think one of the patients must have—"

"We will start a search of their rooms, Nola. You"—Honoria turned to the breakfasters—"will please stay here until we have finished."

"I don't know that we will," Mrs. Lowell said. "I, for one, resent being ordered about, especially with the price I'm paying per day!"

"Oh, Mrs. Lowell!" Honoria's voice was honeyed. "We would never *dream* of ordering you to do anything! We only think it would be more convenient for you to stay here while we rummage around in the rooms. I promise we won't disturb anything of yours."

Alison was amused to see Toby sneak behind Honoria's back and disappear. Honoria would be furious at that!

In a minute only Mrs. Lowell, Mr. Keene, and Alison were left in the dining room.

Mrs. Lowell smothered a giggle and then could not repress a very broad wink at Alison. Alison winked back. She laughed gaily about Honoria's combined anger and discomfiture. Even Mr. Keene had a half smile on his face.

"They certainly started a tempest in a bouillon cup," he said with unexpected humor. "I shouldn't laugh," he added.

"Please, Mr. Keene, don't fight it," Mrs. Lowell said.

"Me fight? I couldn't fight a gnat!"

"I mean we *should* laugh. A good laugh these days is hard to find. All due respect and sorrow for Frank Newman—still, we must go on, mustn't we?"

"Mrs. Lowell," Alison said, "you seem to dislike the doctor and the nurse and Honoria, too. Why do you stay here if you feel this way?"

"Dear, I get my jollies by trying their patience. Every week one or the other of them tries to con me into signing a life-long tenancy. They promise eternal care, perpetual vigilance as to my well-being, all for willing the Honoria Nursing Home my worldly goods when I expire. And each week I pretend my resistance is lessening. They get so hopeful and then so disheartened. I'm like a cat playing with a mouse and I should be ashamed, but I revel in it."

Alison's face had paled. "Mrs. Lowell, I have a very dreadful suspicion that Mr. Newman died because he had signed those papers. Do you think—"

"Of course, I think so. He was old and

feeble and had very little time to live, anyway, but I'm convinced he was helped along to his demise. It's happened before."

"Then why hasn't someone been notified? If they are murdering people—"

"Oh, it's not as bad as that, young lady," Mr. Keene said. "Murder is a nasty word."

Alison said, "Yes, isn't it? The police or the A.M.A. should be informed. This is the most inhuman treatment I've ever heard of, and I shall take it upon myself to—to—"

"What proof have you, dear?" Mrs. Lowell asked. "Perhaps, if you get any proof, you can do something. Now mind you, it's only *old* people they try to influence. Otherwise, this is a perfectly legitimate nursing home. Look at *you*, look at Joe, look at Toby. Nobody would try to con you. Your life spans are too long. Ah, here's Miss Thermometer again."

"You are free to go to your rooms, if you wish," Nola said, ignoring Mrs. Lowell with a toss of her head.

"Did you find the bouillon cup?" Mr. Keene asked.

Nola didn't answer.

Alison got a jacket from her room. Then she went outside. The sun had warmed the air a bit and she needed to be alone by the sea. The distress and horror inspired by the nursing home were enormous. She had to do something! Always, when she decided on a course of action, when she knew exactly what she wanted, she went after it with alacrity. But what action could she take now?

There was a sudden little chill to the air, but its freshness helped to clear Alison's mind. She had no idea what she could do about the dreadful events that were evidently a continuing routine at the Honoria Nursing Home. She knew that without proof of any criminal action, she would be helpless. How to get proof? She walked fast as her mind galloped from one impractical idea to another.

Oh, Joe, Joseph! she thought. Where are you when I need you so badly?

She was aware that she had kept one devastating thought strictly away from serious consideration. It was too destructive. But it kept forcing itself to the edge of her mind and at last she had to face it.

Her father. Her beloved Daddy. Had he been helped along to his death? But it couldn't be—they'd known of his daughter's existence and therefore realized he wouldn't will his estate to them. She felt white-hot tears blinding her eyes.

Alison shook herself and walked even faster. Her pace was close to jogging and, as she covered the bare ground, she became aware of something buried so deep in her mind that she couldn't get at it. It kept sliding out of reach. It was something frightening that struggled to get free but was still secreted in the depths of her consciousness.

A crawling, icy terror abruptly widened her eyes until they were dark pools in her white face. Suddenly she knew what her dread was.

Supposing her father had left his estate to the nursing home in case he had no survivors. That—plus the business last night—could very well mean *she* was in great danger. She must flee this place at once. She must demand the distributor head for her car and leave. But then their inhuman practices could go on without

anybody doing anything to put them out
of business.

No, she must stick it out, must be
watchful and constantly careful. Her only
immediate course of action would be to go
to the other bed patients and try to warn
them without frightening the living day-
lights out of them.

Despite the fear that was flooding her
body, Alison felt better for her decision.
Perhaps she could prevent another...
murder. That was what it was, no matter
how adamantly Mr. Keene refused to accept the word.

The fear that had gripped her for a few
minutes turned into a blind fury. Alison
refused to be intimidated. She would put
up a fight.

Just then she saw Frampton coming toward her in a hurry. Her heart did a little
Highland fling of joy. Joe was back! The
big brown dog galloped up, holding a piece
of driftwood in his mouth and dropping it
at her feet. He waited expectantly, want-
ing it thrown back to him, of course. But
Alison looked at it carefully and her heart
contracted. It was *her* piece of driftwood,

the piece she had left in the cellar. She could easily recognize the shape, the markings, and the color.

That meant—that meant that it was quite possible Joseph Lansing had been her attacker last night.

Chapter Seven

Alison told herself: He tried to hurt me—Joe actually tried to hurt me! He doesn't love me at all. His kisses were pretend. He's probably in cahoots with the nursing-home criminals. No, he isn't. He was angry about the sedative in the bouillon. But still, he hurt me and he doesn't love me. He's probably laughing at me this very minute. No, he isn't. He mustn't be! What is he? Who is he? Is he an enemy or an ally?

Her thoughts stuck like spurs into her brain.

When she returned from her walk and

entered the home, the doctor was there. He talked in a mellow, oiled voice as he asked about everyone's health.

When he examined Alison, his smile broadened.

"You look distraught," he said. "Lovely in your dishevelment, but not at all well."

"That's what I like about you, Doctor. Your soothing bedside manner!"

"Perhaps it's your sharpness that has sent both our young men away," the doctor said, not quite as smoothly as before.

"What do you mean?"

"Joseph Lansing and Toby Weston. Neither of them are here. They've flown the coop."

"Joe is here," Alison said. "I just saw his dog." Her voice was coming over a lump in her throat.

"Go look out the back, my dear. Joseph's car is missing. He's a brash young man, and I'm not sure I'll accept him as a patient anymore."

Alison had no words to refute the doctor's statement. She was confused, hurt, and unwilling to argue about anything, true or untrue.

She went downstairs and to the back of the house to find Sam, the handyman.

As she passed the room that had been Joe's, she looked in hopefully, but there was no sign of any occupation. Why should she be hopeful? she scolded herself. Joe was treacherous. She had loved him, but now she must banish him from her heart.

"Sam!" she called from outside the staff's rooms. "Sam, I'd like to talk to you a minute."

Sam opened his door and smoothed his hair. "Yes, Miss Munro. What can I do for you?"

"You can return the distributor head to my car, Sam! It was wicked of you to take it. I want it back. Now! I need to go to my cottage in Fairview."

"Sorry, miss. I removed it because I was ordered to and I gave both yours and young Lansing's to Mrs. Stevens."

"Mr. Lansing's car has left. Did you give him back his distributor head?"

"No, indeed. He must have bought another while he was away and put it in when he came back."

"Did you see him, Sam?" Alison asked.

"No, ma'am."

"Will you go look under the hood of my car and see if he was nice enough to replace mine, too."

"Yes, ma'am." Sam went out the back door and within minutes was back, shaking his head.

"No, Mr. Lansing didn't put a new one in yours."

"Thanks for looking, Sam."

And thank *you*, Joseph, for your thoughtfulness, blast you! she thought. Alison was rigid with anger. There's no fool like a young fool in love, she added sourly to herself.

The front room was the scene of spurious cheeriness. Dr. Pitt was sitting in the most comfortable chair, exhaling smoke through his nostrils and looking like a fat, petulant dragon.

Honoria was there, holding a sheaf of papers in one hand and waving the other to emphasize her words to the doctor. The words were low and seemingly confidential.

Mr. Keene sat on the edge of his chair,

smiling uneasily. "I wonder," he said musingly, "if one can become senile without being aware of it."

"Your best friends wouldn't tell you," Mrs. Lowell said rather acidly although her face was merry enough.

Alison entered the room purposefully and stopped in front of Honoria.

"Mrs. Stevens, I want the distributor head replaced in my car's engine. I have to make a short visit to my cottage in Fairview. Will you see that it's put back immediately."

Honoria came out of her chair with what might be called a snarl of annoyance.

"Again!" she remonstrated. "Am I never to be free of your complaints and your fermenting trouble?"

"There, there, Honoria," the doctor said. "You mustn't let yourself become perturbed, my dear. Stay calm like me. Alison dear, what seems to be the trouble *now?*"

"The trouble now is that I want to drive into Fairview, but my car won't start. Sam removed a necessary part on the orders of Mrs. Stevens and says she is the one who has it. I want it, and I want it now!"

"My dearest girl," the doctor said in his oiliest voice, "what are you thinking of? You have a strange look on your face."

"Nothing printable, that's what I'm thinking of."

"You know that you must stay quietly here to rest, to eat well, and to recover your strength. You simply must not traipse around in your car, get tired, and reopen the small lesion on your lung."

His smile was all teeth.

"You're telling me the distributor head won't be returned to me. You're saying I'm virtually a prisoner, aren't you?"

"Now, now! Excitement is very bad for you, Alison. I have to tell you—"

She stopped him with a bitter laugh, turned around, and went outside.

She wore no head covering and let her hair tangle in the wind, not caring when she sloshed through puddles. The sun was hidden, and a fat white sea gull squatted on a cliff. He looked at her with cold, incurious eyes. She said hello to the bird and watched it take off with a squawk.

Alison wished she could take off, too.

She speculated about walking to Fairview. That was obviously what Joe had done. Maybe Toby, too. But it was possible that when Joe got his car started, he gave Toby a lift. What shabby treatment Joe had given *her!* The beast!

Later she thought again about walking to Fairview. It would really be quite a little hike. Maybe she'd try it tomorrow or the next day. Why was it necessary that she go to Fairview? she asked herself. Was it just to get away? That, yes. And also to pick up a distributor head at a garage, to find a flashlight in her cottage, and to show independence and disobey the nursing home's rules. She wanted the flashlight for another foray into the cellar. With a light she wouldn't be surprised by an attacker.

She still found it hard to believe that Joe was the one who had hit her. But Frampton's possession of her driftwood weapon did seem to prove his guilt.

That night a stab of homesickness shot through Alison. She needed to go back to Aiken, but to be in Aiken without her father—tears came to her eyes. She felt deprived of love. She felt utterly alone and friendless. Then with a surge of disgust she made herself stop indulging in maudlin self-pity. Pillows salted with tears were not for her!

There was a slithering noise in her room and, alarmed, Alison flicked on her bedside lamp.

Sitting up in bed, she carefully looked around. There was nothing to see but the usual furniture. Then her eye caught a gleam of white sticking under the door. A piece of paper?

She retrieved it, took it to the light, and then her heart turned over. It was her father's handwriting. Who could be so cruel, so tormenting and mocking as to do this to her? It took her a moment before she could read.

"'My dearest Lis.'" She had whispered the written words. Lis had been her father's pet name for her. "'You have been sad, dear, and for that I'm terribly sorry. But what I have done, and am doing, is more important than anyone's mourning. Be of good cheer and always hope for the best. All my love to my dear daughter.'" It was signed by her dad.

It had to be a letter he'd written before his death. It couldn't mean he was still alive, could it? Of course not. She'd buried his poor emaciated body in the family plot in Aiken. But—but—what if he... No, don't be foolish, Alison! she chided herself. She turned the paper over. Down in the bottom left-hand corner were the words, "Don't rock the boat!"

Her rage was monumental. Joseph! It was *he* who was tormenting her! How could any decent human being copy a dead man's handwriting just to cause anguish, to torment someone he had encouraged to love him? Joe was as slippery as a snake!

Alison was sitting upright in a sort of catatonic state when the pitiful cries for help sounded through the vent in her bathroom.

The anger she felt, plus the urge to do something decisive and active, got her off her bed and into a warm bathrobe. Alison wouldn't wait till she had a flashlight. She knew who her enemy was and she would challenge him when he approached her in the cellar. This time she would find the source of the cries for help no matter how often she was hit on the head.

She'd be prepared this time—not with weapons but with expectancy. Despite her brave, imprudent heedlessness, Alison carried a high-heeled slipper in one hand. A sharp heel could make an adversary sorry.

On the way down the stairs, Alison heard no sound but her own breathing and the thump of her heart. Flickering shadows made witchlike forms on the walls. She reminded herself that shadows are always worse than realities.

One small noise behind her was all the warning she got. She felt herself pushed. Then she was pitching down the remaining steps, hurling into a newel post and seeing a great many stars of different colors.

"Here! What's this? What's this? How— oh, an accident!" The doctor's voice sounded, echoed, and re-echoed in Alison's throbbing head. "Help, someone! Help me get her back to her bed! Honoria, yes, and Mr. Keene? Thanks. You take her shoulders. I'll take..." The voice faded as Alison lost consciousness again.

The next thing Alison knew, she was in her bed and the doctor was hovering over her. The nurse stood nearby.

"How do you feel?" the doctor asked.

"Great! I love bleeding!"

"You're not bleeding, dear. At least, not anymore. There's only a small cut on your shoulder."

"Who pushed me?"

"Now, Alison, please no melodrama! You tripped on your long robe. Nobody pushed you, silly girl!"

Alison controlled her impatience. She knew very well she had been pushed and she knew why. She was "rocking the boat" again and some member of the staff wouldn't have it. It could have been Honoria, Nola, Nancy, Rose, or even the doctor. Mustn't forget Dr. Luther Pitt or Sam, the handyman. And while you're at it, Alison, include Joseph Lansing, the snake.

"Now," said the doctor, "let's see if there's anything injured and how our ribs are."

Nothing was injured and our ribs were sound.

"We'll let you sleep now, dear," the doctor said. "Come, Nola, we'll let our patient be. We'll check her in the morning."

They tiptoed out of the room.

Reaction set in then. Alison's lip trembled and she had to lock her fingers together to keep them from shaking.

When a soft knock sounded on her door, she garnered enough strength to say, "Go away!"

The door opened anyway and in the light from her bedside table she saw Joseph Lansing.

"Not *you!*" Alison snarled. "Haven't you done me enough damage? Haven't you battered me? Haven't you hurt me to the quick by copying my father's writing? How can you be such a rat?"

"Hush, darling, keep your voice down. I'm not supposed to be here, you know."

"Yes, I know. I also know you've been back here to knock me out in the cellar and to push me down the stairs. Yes, indeed, I know!"

"You know what I like about you, Alison? Your warm and trusting nature! I didn't knock you out or push you down! I'm the guy who loves you! I wouldn't hurt you for the world! You know that very well."

Alison would have given a lot to believe him. But, "I don't understand you," she said.

"I'm an enigma," he stated.

"You're a pain in the neck," she answered, but her heart went out to him because his face had a tight expression and his eyes were worried.

She mustn't go soft, she warned herself. That cute little-boy smile held a mouthful of tiger's teeth.

"I have to disappear again, darling. Have faith in me, please." He kissed her cheek and left.

He vanished as softly as he'd come and Alison lost herself in mists of meditation.

Chapter Eight

As soon as Joe had disappeared, dozens of questions popped into Alison's mind. He'd only been with her a very short time, but couldn't she have cleared up some of the mysteries that continued to bother her? Why hadn't she asked him if he knew anything about the note purportedly from her father? He'd denied hitting her in the cellar and pushing her down the stairs.

Why was he in hiding? What did he know about the nightly cries for help? Did he know who her enemy was if it wasn't he himself?

She was suddenly very, very tired of boggling her mind with unanswerable questions. She was living in a sort of soap opera: Tune in tomorrow to find out if Alison survives the night and finds happiness. The day and night had been like a wire pulled tight, full of expectancy and tension.

Weak with emotional fatigue, Alison finally fell into a deep sleep and woke up to a gray day. What an ending to the summer! Rain, thunder, and more rain. She got up and looked out the window.

Gulls whooped and dipped. The sky had a yellowish cast and a ground swell had begun to build up.

By the time she had showered and dressed in her gray slacks and a lavender sweater, the rain was coming down in wind-driven sheets.

Mrs. Lowell was sounding off, as usual, when Alison joined the group for breakfast.

"Just because he has a caduceus on his bumper, that doctor's insignia, he thinks he's the father of medicine," she said about her favorite subject, Luther Pitt. "*You* know the type. Easily identified—family doctor, friend of the folks, a put-on personality. 'This medicine may taste bad, dear, but it's just what you need. Drink it down like a good girl.' His expression serious, concerned, noble. Yish!"

Alison's mood was greatly lightened by Mrs. Lowell's chastisement of Dr. Pitt. The old woman was an outspoken, humorous, and refreshing virago whose very sourness made life at the nursing home almost fun.

"You *do* carry on," Mr. Keene said to Mrs. Lowell. There was neutrality in his voice, as if he didn't want to be caught with his thoughts showing.

Honoria bustled in. "How are we all this morning?" she gushed. "How splendid we look! Refreshed, looking well-slept, looking ready for our bouillon!"

"We've gone through this before, Mrs. Stevens," Alison said, and her voice was calm and mild. "Surely it doesn't need repeating every day?"

"No, no! I forgot! Coffee for our *star* boarder!"

"You are right. Thank you." Alison was exceedingly polite, but there was a naughty glimmer in her clear blue eyes. "Uh, Mrs. Stevens, do you have the papers concerning my father's death?"

"I believe Dr. Pitt has all that, although why you should have such a macabre interest, I'll never know." She looked hesitant. Then, "I'll be back," she added.

"I'll try to conceal my impatience." Mrs. Lowell's wicked murmur brought another smile to Alison.

"Well!" Mr. Keene exclaimed. "Look who just blew in!"

"Toby!" Alison cried. "How nice to have you back!"

Toby was wearing large tinted glasses, which covered his mild brown eyes and partly concealed the dark smudges of fatigue beneath them.

"Just in time for your beef broth, young man," Mrs. Lowell said, "and perhaps you'll be allowed a piece of toast, too! Our Honoria doesn't like her pets to be AWOL, you know, and she *might* send you to bed without breakfast!"

Toby forced a smile, but it had all the humor of a denture ad.

"Alison," he said, "if you've finished your coffee, will you meet me outside?"

"It's raining, or didn't you notice?" Mr. Keene said. "Young men should have more consideration for young ladies than to—"

"Yes," Alison interrupted, "I'll meet you on the porch, Toby. Just let me get a raincoat."

In a few minutes she joined Toby on the sheltered side of the porch.

"Gosh, what a day!" Alison said. "You look very serious, Toby. Where have you been, or don't you want to tell me?"

"Alison, I need your help." Toby's voice was hoarse with exhaustion. "When I told you I had no family, I wasn't telling the truth. I have an aunt, or maybe I should say I *had* an aunt. This aunt was a very special person. I loved her. I've been in Fairview and in the three other towns within reasonable distance, trying to find out where she is or whether she ever *left* this establishment they call the Honoria Nursing Home."

Alison felt numbed with an icy portent of calamity. Toby's words all tied in with the twist of fear she experienced whenever she let her dread suspicions surface. The fingers of her folded hands were agitated and there was repressed emotion in her face.

"Was she a patient here, Toby?" she asked in a tone barely above a whisper.

"No. She was a nurse."

Then Alison said, "Toby, there—there was a nurse here when my father—I mean, the nurse before Nola. She was so nice. Her name was Gertrude Smith."

Toby nodded violently. "That's her. That's my aunt. She was the nicest, kindest person." He went on and on. His mild raving was almost mechanical. It was like the failure of an electric circuit, a loose connection somewhere, and Alison realized it was because of an almost total exhaustion.

"Toby, stop!" she ordered, taking his arm firmly. "You must go to bed and stay there until you're over your fatigue. We'll talk about this later and you can count on me to help."

"All right, Alison. I'm not making much sense, I know. I'll rest. Then we *will* solve it, won't we? I haven't had any sleep at all since I left here. I—I . . ." His voice dropped into a murmur, and Alison guided him inside and up to his room.

As she was closing the door on him, he had one more thing to say. "I took the bouillon cup from Frank Newman's room."

She controlled the impulse to question him about the cup. She was quite sure it had something very important to do with a lot of things.

After going to her room, she went downstairs again and curled up in an easy chair. She had the same old mystery novel in hand, but somehow the book's excitement paled beside the happenings, real and imagined, in the nursing home.

Mrs. Lowell was flipping through a magazine, Mr. Keene was setting up a chess board, preparing to play against himself, and Alison tried to relax. She was planning to visit the three remaining bed patients this morning, but knew that she should wait until Nola and Rose had finished their duties with them.

She remained sitting, holding her open book, but her body was so tense it looked as if she might rocket out of her chair at any moment. In addition to visiting the bed patients, she wanted to explore the cellar again, but this time she would take Toby with her. Toby, when not fatigued, would be a strong ally and would provide protection. Alison had a very positive feeling that the cries in the night came from Toby's aunt, Gertrude Smith. The *nice* nurse.

Honoria came into the front room. Her smile looked as if it hurt her mouth as she greeted her ambulatory patients.

"Did I hear that Toby has come back?" she asked. At Mrs. Lowell's nod, Honoria went on. "Toby and Joseph are prime examples of what young men *shouldn't be*. Weak and self-indulgent, chronic complainers, and quite childish. Don't you agree, Alison? I'm sure you're used to attention from men. What must you think of these two unlikely specimens?"

Alison recognized that Honoria was needling her. She didn't blame the woman for that. After all, Alison had undermined Honoria's dictatorship time and again. Alison knew quite well that everyone erroneously believed Toby to be sissified, but she was also sure that no one could put Joe into the same category. Honoria plainly wanted Alison to be mad enough to do something that would force the doctor to expel her from the home.

Instead of being shaken with anger at

the irritating woman, Alison was filled
with disgust.

There was a moment when the tension
in the room was as powerful as an electric
charge, but Mrs. Lowell broke the spell.

"What nonsense you do talk," she said
to Honoria. "What drivel! Aha, here comes
Miss Thermometer with news, no doubt,
that someone wouldn't drink their beef
broth. Bully for them!"

"Mrs. Lowell," Honoria said in a voice
that might have been used in dealing with
an idiot, "may I remind you that Miss
Nola Brown is a registered nurse and as
such is owed appropriate respect? Your
calling her Miss Thermometer is quite in-
fantile, childish, and rude."

"Tut-tut," Mrs. Lowell said. "I stand re-
buked. I hope Miss Thermometer will forgive my uncouth words." She rose from
her chair in awful dignity and stalked out
of the room.

Alison swallowed the chuckle that almost burst from her lips and was starting
to leave also, but Honoria turned to her,
a fearsome scowl on her face.

"We had *no* insubordination until *you*

came here," she said grimly. "You have brought out all sorts of underlying, intractable rebelliousness. I wish you would pack up and leave!"

"Have Sam put back my distributor head then," Alison answered. "When I have finished one or two projects around here, I'll be only too happy to depart!"

"Doctor won't allow it. I was just expressing a wish, not a probability." Honoria followed Nola out of the room.

When they had disappeared into Honoria's private quarters, Alison decided the time had come to warn the three remaining bed patients. She was very quiet, almost to the point of being stealthy, as she went from room to room. To her disappointment, all three were deep in their drug-induced sleep. How frustrating it was to have her warning well rehearsed in terms not to frighten the patients— and then not be able to deliver it.

She wondered if Toby had had enough rest. She would like to formulate plans with him. She still wanted him to go with her to the cellar. She needed him to bolster her shaky nerves. She would rather

have Joe, but Joe was like a mirage—
sometimes there but mostly *not*.

Suddenly she remembered he'd said he
loved her. She couldn't keep back a surge
of happiness at the memory despite his
disappearing act.

Oh, Joe, I'm afraid I love you, too, she
thought. Come back! Help me! Help me
find the despicable coward who pretended
to be my father with that copied handwriting in the letter. Help me find the
source of the cries in the night.

Very softly she opened Toby's door. If he
were still asleep, she wouldn't disturb him,
poor, tired young man.

He was not there.

Was everybody she counted on going to
be as elusive as a wisp of fog? Joe disappeared when most wanted and now
Toby—when she needed him to accom-
pany her down to the cellar—had vanished like a puff of smoke. There must be
something about her that made young
men flee when they were required for support. Maybe they felt she was too pushy,
too aggressive, something like that.

If young men actually thought she was

too efficient, too self-confident, and too utterly practical, then—well, *she* could admire the cool head and stout heart that had helped her to fight her own battles even if others couldn't.

That decided, she went downstairs for the purpose of invading the cellar. She had no weapon and no flashlight, but it was daylight now and the demons of night would not haunt the ghostly place.

Alison had failed to reckon with the staff. Not only was the cook, Nancy, fiddling with a crate of something near the cellar door, but Sam, the handyman, actually had his chair leaning back against it.

"Something we can do for you, miss?" Nancy asked.

"No, thank you. Oh, but, yes. I'd like a stronger reading light in my room," Alison quickly added.

"Rose is the one to ask," Sam said without getting to his feet. He wasn't exactly impolite but seemed determined not to be helpful.

Alison turned and went to the front room without another word.

She was in time to hear Mrs. Lowell say, "She has the build of a giraffe and the mind of a sheep!"

Thank goodness for Mrs. Lowell. The old lady's envenomed tongue made Alison's resentments seem petty and unimportant.

An abrupt doubt of her own abilities caused her much uneasiness at this moment, but she resolved to invade the cellar again after the staff was safely abed.

She knew that things that look bad during the daytime look infinitely worse at night. Yet she had no choice. She must try to enter the cellar later.

She quite hated the idea—someone wished her out of the way and might go to the trouble of doing her harm. But she had to investigate the cries in the night. Then there was the mystery of the note in her father's writing. And now there was Toby's statement that *he* had taken Frank Newman's bouillon cup. That might mean something *very* important.

She wondered if she looked the way she felt—as if someone had switched off all the courage inside her.

Chapter Nine

Alison thought the nursing home was as still as death. Then she told herself that that was not a happy way of putting it.

Let's not think of anything unpleasant, she mentally added. Be positive, be cheerful. Not easy? Now listen to me, Alison, she ordered herself. There's no written guarantee that life is going to go the way you want it to. We just have to deal with it, bad or good. Now get on with it!

She hated to leave her cozy bed. She told herself that the cries for help had not

sounded this night and so she could postpone—oh, don't be such a coward!

She could hear another storm coming
out of the north, thunder sounding like a
giant bowling ball rolling down an ech-
oing alley. It was just the kind of night to
luxuriate under the covers and feel sorry
for those not so snug.

But she mustn't be milksoppy. She
squared her shoulders, and forced herself
out of bed and into jeans, sweater, and
sneakers. Now to face the trip to the cellar
and then to start the search for Gertrude
Smith. Alison was quite sure the cries
came from an imprisoned Gertrude—but
what if she were wrong?

"Oh, Daddy," she whispered, "what
should I do?" She expected no answer and
none was given.

As she crept from her room, down the
stairs, and to the back of the house, she
kept her mind off her project. Instead she
thought of Joe. Loving him was both pleasure and pain, delight and deprivation,
dreamy and disappointing. Like the waves
in the ocean, love built itself up and then
tumbled down. So quickly did it surge up

and back, one knew there had been no proper foundation laid.

Enough of Joe! Now she must concentrate on her task.

The cellar door was slightly ajar, and the dim light was on. Did that mean someone was down there? Alison listened intently for any sounds. When none reached her ears, she decided that the open door and the light were due to carelessness. However, she took great pains to descend the cellar stairs noiselessly.

The furnace and hot-water heater loomed up like old friends. It was beyond them that she had been clobbered. And that was where she must go now, testing every door, looking in every corner and behind every crate.

She ordered herself to take control, to stop hearing ghosts and seeing shadows. She forced down her nauseated panic and took deep breaths. She told herself there was nothing threatening her, and even if there were, she'd be prepared this time to hit back.

As Alison crept deeper into the murk, she made herself think of some more trivia. Things like her father laughing at her and telling her a lady doesn't hit to maim. A woman's slap was supposed to discipline the male victim, not cause unconsciousness. That had been when a rude boy had teased her and she'd fought back. Devastatingly.

She smiled at the memory and attempted to open a door to her left. It was stiff at first but then swung wide with a screech of rusty metal. She froze and listened. Nothing.

There was a tiny glimmer of light coming through a grated window, enough so she could see she was in a deserted laundry room with large tubs. A laundry room that had not been used in ages.

Softly she closed the door and explored the rest of the cellar. There were dusty old steamer trunks left here and there, as if to impede her progress. A crate of empty wine bottles rattled alarmingly when she tripped on it. And then there was another door whose knob caught a gleam from the faraway light bulb. That meant it was used. Otherwise, it would have been covered with dust. Perhaps she had discovered Gertrude's prison.

Alison tried the knob and suddenly the world went crazy with spinning lights and no air to breathe. She was aware of something being slung over her head, then a sharp blow just above her nose, a nosebleed, and somebody dragging her, throwing her down, and slamming a door. Then blackness descended, and there was nothing.

Alison awoke with a feeling of disorientation. The unfamiliar place was too small, too still and dark. Where was she? Certainly not in her comfortable room. There was a faint odor of decay mixed unpleasantly with an equally faint odor of lye.

Very carefully Alison lifted her swimming head and looked for something, *anything*, that would clear up her confusion. Unsteadily she got to her feet. They felt a mile or so below her body, but she took a few tottering steps.

She ran into a cold, wet wall almost at once. In another direction, she came up against a door. A door that was securely fastened, locking her in, she knew immediately. That fact sharpened her muddled mind. She turned around, staying in one place so she wouldn't run into any more solid obstructions, and made her eyes focus again.

She saw, at last, an indistinct glimpse of dull light through a grating and under it two laundry tubs. Now she knew where she was. Knowing her location didn't mean she could leave it. She tried the door again but found it would not move.

She left the door, climbed up on one of the tubs, and tried the grating. It was more than grating—there were iron bars implanted sturdily in the cement of the walls. Escape was impossible. But she must get out! She was convinced that the door she had tried, the one with the pol- ished knob, must be Gertrude's prison, and it was imperative she free the nurse be- fore something bad happened to her. Alison was quite sure that something ter- rible was in store for Gertrude—she had no information to that effect, but the feel- ing was so strong she had to do something. Where was Toby? If she cried out, loud and strong, would she be heard?

Just then the old familiar cries came to

her ears. The cries were near, becoming louder, more urgent. They burst in, filling the laundry room, then died with a sob.

"Gertrude!" Alison cried. "Gertrude, can you hear me?"

Only silence answered her. She tried again and again to call to Gertrude. Then she knocked on the walls and beat on the floor with a scrubbing board she'd tripped over. There was no response and there were no more cries.

As Alison paced her small cell, she became aware of a latticework grating underfoot. It undoubtedly covered a drain for the laundry.

She knelt down and felt it all over. To her surprise, the latticework was not too heavy and came up in her hands. What was there underneath? Might it be a drain wide enough for her slender body to slip through? And where did it go? Most drains emptied into the ocean, she knew. She'd been horrified to see garbage thrown to the sea from the top of the cliffs but was soon pacified when she saw gulls catch it all while it was still in the air.

Her head felt heavy and dizzy when she

lowered it to the drain, but she thought she detected a fresh, salty waft of air coming up. That meant the drain opened onto the cliffs. Alison believed that the opening was above the sea. Otherwise, there wouldn't be this fresh ozone wafting at her.

The cliffs didn't hold any terror for her. Many a summer she'd scrambled down and then up cliffs all over this area. There was a worry, however, that daunted her. What if she entered the drain, then got stuck? If only she had something to help her.

There must be something here in the old laundry that she could make use of. Her head was still woozy and schemes drifted around her mind without making any sense. She got up and started feeling her way along the oozing walls.

What Alison was looking for she didn't know, but when she felt a rusty hook under one hand, an idea jelled. If there were hooks, there might be laundry lines. And if the rope wasn't too ancient and rotted, she could use it. If only there were light to see with!

The glimmer from outside was almost

gone. Was this the "darkest before the dawn" phenomenon? Alison had no idea how long she'd been locked in.

She almost missed the coiled rope that lay swathed in cobwebs in a corner.

Her mind was made up. She refused to tamely wait in this dungeon until the ones upstairs decided she was no longer a nuisance. She would escape and face her enemies.

As Alison uncoiled the rope, hoping there were no spiders among the webs, she tested it for strength. It seemed to be made of heavy fiber. It would do. It would have to do!

One end she tied securely in a square knot around the sturdy underpinning of the laundry tubs, and the other end went round her waist. She felt quite secure knowing that if the drain became too narrow she could pull herself up by the rope.

Now her hands examined the drain by feel. When it had been in use, slime had undoubtedly coated it, but it was dry and smooth now.

Feet first, she lowered herself inch by inch.

As she descended, the drain lost its

smoothness and narrowed. Her rubber-soled sneakers kept her from going too fast. And for a while she was almost horizontal. And then the drain opened into another drain and she was able to squirm around to a head-first position.

That was better than blindly backing down into the unknown. There was a pale glow ahead of her that might be her exit to freedom. But she must be careful now. The slant of the drain had suddenly become steep and Alison had to cling to the rough, rocky walls and brace her sneakered feet to keep from plunging down. Although the drain had not narrowed enough to restrict her passage, it had torn her clothes, scraped her elbows, and bruised her everywhere.

A sound that was not the pounding of the surf came to her and she halted her descent and listened. Voices? Men's voices? Were her ears playing tricks on her? The sounds were muffled and rather hollow in tone—completely unfamiliar and unintelligible. If her impressions were correct, and the sounds were made by men, were they enemies or friends? She must keep her downward passage slow. She had to see these people before they saw her.

The light was stronger now. It wasn't natural light—it flickered too much. A candle would flicker, or maybe a fire.

Alison let herself slip down two more feet. It was most uncomfortable with her sore hands clutching the ragged walls, her feet and legs spread apart to keep from plunging, her nose bleeding, and her head thumping.

And then she saw the silhouettes of three figures. Their backs were toward her. The candle gave no more than a dim view of masculine forms, but there was one that made her heart stand still. She must be hallucinating, dreaming. The blow to her head had affected her brain.

Then his voice drifted up to her.

"Daddy!" she cried and fell the rest of the way into the cave.

To say the men were startled would be an understatement. One fell over backward, one gasped, and the other swore.

Then all three rushed over to pick her up.

"Alison," they all exclaimed.

"Alison, dear heavens! Where did you come from? How do you feel?" Joe asked.

Dazedly Alison tried to answer. "Firecrackers are exploding in my head and it's no great pleasure to breathe. Otherwise, I'm in tip-top shape. Except"—she paused—"I'm afraid I've lost my mind. I actually think I'm seeing my father. But he's dead. I buried him. Does that mean I'm dead, too?"

"Lis, darling, you're not dead and neither am I. I'll have to explain later." Her father kissed her bruised cheek, smoothed her hair, and used his handkerchief on her bloody nose. "Right now we're too busy planning. Be patient with us, dear."

Alison was too numbed to think. She looked at the other two men and was not even surprised to see that one was Joseph Lansing and the other Toby Weston.

Her body seemed strangely light, as if suspended in air, and for a minute there she turned an interesting shade of green.

"Watch out," Joe exclaimed. "I think she's going to pass out!"

"I am not," Alison snapped. Then her face began to twitch and slowly tears began to form in her eyes and spill over. She didn't make faces when she cried—just a faint twitching and then the overflow of tears.

"I'm so tired," she whispered. "All I want now is my bed. Come to think of it, *any* bed would do. The floor of the cave is beginning to look good to me!"

Her father walked her gently to the back of the cave and sat her down on a sleeping bag.

"This is mine, Lis dear," he said. "Rest now and we'll talk later. Poor child, poor girl! I'm so sorry I've caused you misery, but I'll make it up to you."

His voice got softer and softer, more and more soothing. Her eyes closed and she slept.

Sunshine was pouring into the mouth of the cave when Alison woke up. She was alone. She found her thoughts going round in circles, but then a scrap of memory spun out of the circles. She had fallen into the cave, probably landing on her head. Because of the blow, she'd imagined her father was alive and that Joe and Toby were

with him. It had been a dream, hadn't it?
It had been a wishful fantasy concocted
by her damaged head.

But...but she was tucked into a sleeping bag! How? Whose? It was too much.

What was she to believe?

Alison felt herself losing consciousness
again. She hoped that more sleep would
loosen some of the knots pulling so tight
inside her, and maybe she'd wake up to
sanity.

Chapter Ten

It was hunger that woke Alison up the second time. She ached in all her joints, and getting to her feet was a painful procedure. She was all by herself in a nice clean cave, but she wouldn't let too many conjectures into her mind. She kept her thoughts at bay. She was afraid if she started surmising, reckoning, and remembering, she'd froth at the mouth like a crazy dog and bite someone. Still, she had to cling to the memory—or was it a delusion?—of her father here in the cave. How real he had seemed to be. She hadn't imagined him. And the sleeping bag! That

127

was real, too. All the same, she knew her father was dead.

Alison shook her head and tried to tidy herself up. Her clothing was all tattered and mussed. She was glad she couldn't see her face—probably a swollen nose, certainly a lump on her forehead, and surely her eyes were circled by black and blue. A pretty sight.

But now she must plan her next move— her exit from the cave and her entrance to the nursing home. She looked forward to facing Honoria. It seemed impossible that that dreadful woman could be the one who had knocked her out and dragged her into the laundry, but Alison was convinced that it was on Honoria's orders that it had been done.

She went to the entrance of the cave. It was halfway down the cliff, and she looked at the boiling cauldron of ocean below. She'd have to wait for the next low tide. White rollers were scudding in to spend themselves on the rocky shore, sucking at the narrow sand bars that were barely visible now. A glimmer of sun peeked through the bleak sky, gilding the spume.

The sharp fangs of the rocky coast lurked just under the surface to rip the bottom out of any boat that dared to venture close.

Alison must keep her soul in patience — a scramble *up* these abutting, slippery cliffs would be foolhardy. She must wait till she could walk to a familiar place where the cliffs were less vertical and where she knew there were footholds. In past years she'd played along that very spot.

Was that how Joe and Toby and her father had gone? There she went again, believing her mad fantasies!

She settled down to wait the change of tides. If only when things happened, she mused, there was time to think! Now, when there was too much time to think, nothing happened. It was particularly wearisome to control her thoughts when her very blurred memory kept picturing her beloved father.

She made Joe come into her mind. That wasn't difficult. She recalled his "almost" declaration of love and her heart skipped a beat. Liar, thought Alison, infuriating, deceitful, beloved liar! But wouldn't it be wonderful if—oh, be gentle with me, my imagination! I'm liable to lose my mind completely. She dozed off and on, still aware of hunger and of the passing time.

It was close to noon when the tide was sufficiently low. There was a fairly easy track down the face of the cliff from the cave. It had been used a lot, Alison was sure. Footholds had been deepened, handholds made smooth so as not to tear the flesh, and slime had been scrubbed away.

Fifteen minutes of slow descent and she was at the bottom. Looking up, Alison saw the cave was invisible and the height of the cliff was awesome. Nobody would dare to scale it from here if he didn't know the path. She must remember exactly where the cave was, just in case. There was a projection of rock that was white in color. The cave was to the left of it. She wouldn't forget.

She walked, breathing deeply, along the edge of the low tide, her feet in the sucking foam, her mind on how to recognize the place she had climbed up and down during the summers of her childhood.

After a panicky time of wondering if she would be caught by the incoming tide and dashed against the jagged rocks, she found her old path. It wasn't as easy as it had been years ago. From disuse, the footholds and handholds had become sheathed in slimy weed, and some mussels were clinging to the rock, making for painful scratches.

When the top was finally reached and Alison was throwing a leg over the edge, Frampton greeted her ecstatically with great wet licks on her exposed face and whimpers of joy.

Alison pushed him aside with, "Give me room, boy! I know you love me, but let me up. Please!"

He did, but Alison saw the dog was wearing a sly grin on his furry face and then she realized why. Joseph had been watching her awkward climb up the cliff.

When she was safely on top, he gave a great bellow of laughter that roused a few gulls and sent them screaming and wheeling away.

"You think I'm funny, do you?" Alison growled.

"Your face, darling! It has all the colors of the rainbow."

"And that amuses you!" She glared at him. "That's quite enough," she said with as much dignity as she could muster.

"Oh, but I'm not finished yet," Joe said calmly. "You're adorable! You're lovable!"

"Lovable! No, lovable is snub nose, cuddly, giggly, and freckled. And I can tell you, sir, there's nothing further from my intentions than to become cuddly and giggly. Now I'm going back to the nursing home."

The silhouette of the big gray house, stark and forbidding even in the sunlight, suggested a prison. Alison shivered a little.

"No, darling," Joe said. "Don't go back yet. Forgive me for laughing at you. It's because I love you so much, and I always find amusement in the things I love!"

Inside, Alison had been boiling, but his last words calmed her.

"Well, here's something else to make you laugh," Alison said. "I thought for a while that my father was still alive. I thought I saw him last night. I thought you and Toby were with him in a cave. Why aren't you laughing?"

"It's better for you not to know too

much," Joe said. "You are far too inquis-
itive."

"Is that so!" she snapped.

Frampton watched his two favorite people bridling at each other. They acted like
a pair of cats walking stiff-legged, circling
each other with wary belligerence, until
suddenly Joe swept Alison into his arms
and kissed her fervently.

Then he pushed her away and said, "You
know Toby's aunt?"

"Gertrude Smith. Yes! She's in—"

"We know where she is. Toby and your
father are working on her rescue."

"Then I wasn't dreaming! Daddy is
really alive! Oh, Joe! He is! He really is!
I want to see him. I want to see him right
now! Where is he?"

"I was afraid of this," Joe said. "Give in
to you a little, and you demand more. Now
listen carefully and *try* to be a good girl.
Your father, Toby, and I are working on
something very important, and we must
not be interrupted. Yes, Gertrude is part
of it. And if you don't hinder us with your
wild impulses, we may get to the solution
soon."

"Solution of what? Tranquilizers in the

bouillon? Persuasion of dying patients to will their worldly goods to—"

"All that and more. Quite a lot more. Now can we trust you, Alison?"

"Of course, you can trust me. You know very well I'm completely trustworthy."

"Yes, but you're also perverse, darling. Now will you go back to the nursing home and pretend nothing has happened?"

"How the heck can I, Joe? I was whacked on the head and thrown into a laundry room. I'm sure that room is next to Gertrude's prison. Anyway, I escaped through my own cleverness and I want to make the guilty person very nervous."

"I want you to act as if nothing, *nothing*, mind you, has happened." He spoke to her as one might speak to a slightly retarded child. He added, "I want you to remember how I feel about you. I have laid my heart at your feet repeatedly, have I not?"

She laughed. "You're really laying it on thick, and if I weren't so hungry, I'd—"

He reached out and touched her shoulder lightly. It was meant to be a reassuring gesture. But looking at the nursing

home, dark and forbidding, Alison was
not reassured.

"Now, darling," Joe said seriously. "I'm
asking you once again—and this time
please listen—*don't* rock the boat!"

Alison left him and limped toward the
home. She drank in the clean, clear ox-
ygen as though it would nourish her, and
she was able to make a very careful and
silent entrance. She reached her room
without being seen by anyone and made
a quick change of clothes, then applied a
rather thick coat of makeup to conceal her
wounds. She then descended the stairs
with a feeling of adventure.

Lovely aromas of food pervaded the air
and Alison thanked her lucky stars she
was in time for lunch.

She saw Honoria sitting at the head of
the table and took a deep breath before
she made an appearance. Honoria looked
like a cat who had been given a big dish
of thick cream. Doubtless the big woman
still thought Alison was locked away in
the old laundry room. That might well be
why she seemed so content.

Mrs. Lowell was talking, as usual. "The

motto for this nursing home," she said sweetly, "is 'There shall be no pleasure within these walls!'"

"Oh, now, Mrs. Lowell," Honoria said in a syrupy tone of voice, "you say that just to be clever, don't you? You *really* like it here."

"I like it enough to make a diet of fingernails," the spunky old woman retorted. "If you know what I mean."

"I'm afraid I don't," Honoria said. "Rose," she called, "bring the pea soup, please."

Just then Alison made her entrance.

Honoria sprang to her feet and looked like a firecracker about to go off. Mrs. Lowell smiled calmly at the girl and mentioned that she'd been missed at breakfast. Mr. Keene patted the chair next to his and indicated that Alison was to sit there.

Honoria sank back into her seat. She seemed at the point of collapse, her face white, her wild eyes fixed with disbelief and hatred on Alison.

"Yes," Alison said, "I missed breakfast this morning. I had things to do."

"My dear," Mrs. Lowell said, "you don't look too well. Perhaps you go out into the weather too often."

"Perhaps I do," Alison agreed.

She fell upon the pea soup with unbridled enthusiasm and wolfed the hot roll that was passed to her.

Honoria had pasted a smile on her face, but she said nothing.

Mrs. Lowell talked about the doctor's next visit to the home. "If only that man wouldn't wear that appalling spotted tie," she said, "I could put more faith in his healing."

Honoria's smile was beginning to wear thin. It disappeared entirely when she answered Mrs. Lowell.

"Doctor," she said, "is well-known as a superbly dressed man." She was very stern, very sincere. "And he's equally famous as a wonderful man of medicine. You should be honored that you're one of his lucky patients."

"Your loyalty is touching," Mrs. Lowell said, "even though misguided."

"I believe," Honoria said with awful dignity, "I shall have the rest of my meal in my room. I find the atmosphere here not entirely to my liking."

She left and Mrs. Lowell giggled. "My feline instincts got out of hand," she said. "Poor Honoria. She brings out the worst in me."

"She's not bad-looking," Mr. Keene said.

"If she has few wrinkles," Mrs. Lowell stated, "it is because she has few thoughts. But she is besotted with Dr. Luther Pitt, and in my opinion, they deserve each other."

Alison was overcome with the need to sleep in her comfortable bed. She had gotten plenty of sleep in the cave, but now it was as if she'd drunk the nursing home's beef broth.

Oh! In a way she had! The pea soup she'd attacked like a starving child probably had the usual sedative in it. Well, for once she'd relax and enjoy a dreamless, luxurious sleep and let everyone else worry about the goings-on.

Joe had said, "Don't rock the boat," and she wouldn't.

Not yet, anyway. There was the unexplained existence of her father who was

working with Joe and Toby and—and let
them do it, whatever it was.

She fell into bed and was instantly
asleep.

Chapter Eleven

When Alison awoke, she was astonished to find it was the next morning. She'd slept all afternoon, slept through dinner, and then slept all night. That must have been a powerful sedative in yesterday's pea soup, she thought, or else it was because she had been so exhausted. She felt wonderful now, ready to face anything! And she had two things to be happy about. Happy? Ecstatic! Her father was mysteriously alive and Joe loved her.

She bathed and stretched out on top of the bed—not to sleep but to prepare her mind for coming events. There were so many thoughts whirling around in her head she hardly knew where to start. She would like to catalogue the things to be done or to be investigated, but how could she even begin without any knowledge of her father's, Joe's, and Toby's activities? Darn them all for being such secretive plotters! Didn't they know that *she,* being in the home and in touch with its doings, could be a help? She remembered Joe's warning to keep out of everything, to stop rocking the boat. What did *he* know? She was sure she knew more than he. About everything!

She lay on the bed, looking through the window, smelling the fragrant soapiness of her body from the long, hot bath, and getting nowhere in her mind. Maybe breakfast would generate lucid thoughts, and if not breakfast, then a brisk walk in the sea breeze.

Soon she was dressed, in a pleated navy skirt, a white silk blouse, and a navy sweater.

Her face was not nearly as battered as it had been, and she found that a light foundation and a carefully applied coat of

makeup covered most of her colorful
bruises. Her nose and one eye were still
slightly swollen, though, and her joints
felt a bit stiff. Nevertheless, a couple of
eggs and several cups of coffee should fix
her.

As Alison was putting on her walking
shoes, she wondered *why,* if Joe, Toby, and
her father knew where Gertrude was, they
didn't rescue her? What was holding them
back? Why didn't they—oh, it was no use
asking unanswerable questions. If she
could only sit down with one of the three
men and dig out their reasons and their
plans, she'd know what *she* could do to
help.

She went down to breakfast.

"Well, young lady," Mrs. Lowell said,
"we thought you'd deserted us like the
two young men did. We were worried until
Rose reported you were asleep. Asleep all
day! You *must* have been tired! You do
look much better today, dear, and aren't
you glad you didn't miss the doctor's visit?
He couldn't come yesterday and will be
here this morning instead. We should all
send up huzzahs and be joyous, shouldn't

we? His visit will make our day!"

Alison said that her day would indeed be made by the doctor's call. Mrs. Lowell had a way of putting things that pleased Alison. Mr. Keene, on the other hand, was so low-keyed one almost wondered if he were asleep.

As she was buttering her third piece of toast, a vaguely familiar old man tottered into the dining room. Mr. Keene quickly got up and helped the man into a chair. The newcomer was very thin and his white hair was somewhat unkempt.

Alison smiled at him and offered him her toast. "Are you new here, sir?" she asked.

"New?" the oldster chortled in a high-pitched voice. "Not so you could notice it. I've been here for years, years, and years! I've lost count."

Mrs. Lowell whispered to Alison, "He came here just a few weeks before you did. His mind has slipped."

Honoria rushed in. "Mr. Thompson! What do you mean by leaving your room?"

The old man's eyes were like a frightened rabbit's. He stared at Honoria and stopped chewing. He had visibly shrunk.

Honoria looked at Alison, as if it were her fault the old man was eating at the table. Her eyes were two hot coals of suspicion and distrust.

"Come, Mr. Thompson," the tall woman said as she took his thin arm. "Come along back to your nice room where Nola is waiting for you. You're a bad boy, you know. I'll have to tell Doctor on you!"

Honoria's laugh was harsh. It splintered into notes that had an ugly ring.

"Poor old man," Alison said. "He was enjoying his toast so much. Aren't the bed patients ever allowed away from their rooms? I should think the change would do them good."

"*Doctor,*" Mrs. Lowell said, mimicking Honoria, "doesn't believe in doing good to patients. They might stop being patients!"

It was a nice day for a change, and Alison was about to go out for her walk when Dr. Pitt appeared.

There was a look in the doctor's eyes that was not entirely paternal as he clasped Alison's arm in his and asked how his favorite young lady was. Alison's reply was cool but polite and she detached her arm from his firmly.

"I'm going for a walk now, Doctor," she said, "and as I told you before, I'd like to be able to use my car. I want some things from the cottage. I believe I'm cured of whatever I had, and pretty soon I'll be returning to Aiken. Will you please give orders to Sam?"

"Dear girl, I'm sure you're anxious to go home to Aiken, but we musn't rush things, must we? I'll listen to your chest, and we'll discuss your wishes after I've determined your state of health." His eyes were wide and glittering.

A feeling that verged on panic seized Alison. The doctor's words were chilling. Her feet seemed locked to the floor, and there was something stirring inside her, something warning her to get away from the man.

"I—I think I'll go for my walk now." She paused, feeling like a rabbit mesmerized by a snake.

"No, dear, not yet," he said, velvet in his voice. "Let me call Nola, and we'll go to your room where I'll examine you."

Alison bolted. She ran out the front door, across the porch, down the steps, and over to the cliff. There was no reasoning behind her action, only an instant of self-preservation. Something told her if she didn't get away from the doctor, she'd end up like Gertrude—without a drain to escape from.

The fact that her father was somewhere in the vicinity didn't help much. He and Joe and Toby were so busy doing something "important" that they had no time for her. What must the doctor be thinking about her action?

He was probably convinced she'd lost her marbles. He'd probably order restraints when she returned. A straitjacket? Well, maybe she *wouldn't* return! She'd given thought to walking to Fairview before. Why not?

She'd go to her cottage. There was always an extra key in a magnetic container under the back water spout. She turned and headed toward town, her panic soothed and her heart lightened.

Alison felt a little guilty about leaving

Gertrude in her prison, but Toby should
be working on that, and he had the help
of her father and Joe. He did, didn't he?
It was all so confusing.

But one conviction was clear—the doctor was a phony in cahoots with Honoria
and probably the rest of the staff. They
were out to make money from the weak-
ened, tranquilized patients, keeping them
at the home longer than necessary and
conning them into willing their estates to
the home. Did her father know that? Was
that what he was working on?

Alison was walking at a brisk pace,
keeping off the road in case the doctor in
his car should be returning to town, when
she heard running footsteps behind her.
She turned and saw Sam coming toward
her. There was no hiding from him. He
had seen her and there was determination
in his approach.

"What do you want, Sam?" she asked
when he was near.

"You! I'm to bring you back. Doctor's
orders."

"No, I'm going to town. I'm tired of the
nursing home."

"Sure, you are! Aren't we all? But that

doesn't matter. We can't have unbalanced patients roaming the countryside, you know. Now come along. I've got Miss Honoria's station wagon just back a ways."

"Sam, you know very well I'm not unbalanced! I'm not even sick. If you hadn't fixed my car so I couldn't use it, I'd have left long ago. The nursing home is a miserable clink, and you know it is. Now let go of my arm."

"Sorry. My orders are to bring you back. It'll be easier on both of us if you come willingly."

"Well, I won't! I'll fight you all the way."

"I know."

"You know? Was it you who hit me in the cellar? Sam, was it? Are you the one who tends Gertrude? Are you? The one who keeps her locked up? Oh, how could you be so cruel? No, I *won't* go with you! You'll have to knock me out again!"

She didn't expect to be taken at her word, and her surprised pain made her cry out when he twisted her arm behind her back and forced her along the road and into the vehicle.

Alison was speechless with anger and her loss of dignity, but her rage was nothing compared to what she felt after Sam had boorishly pushed her through the front door and into Dr. Pitt's waiting grasp.

"Let me go at once, Doctor," she said icily. "I've been humiliated and treated terribly. This is something I won't stand for. Now let go of me."

"Poor child," the doctor said. "She's raving."

Mrs. Lowell heaved her tea-cozy shape into the front hall. "Let Alison be," she said. "She's not raving, she's angry! And so she should be! Why are you manhandling her?"

"Mrs. Lowell," the doctor said, "please mind your own business. This poor, deranged girl had become psychotic. If you wish to be helpful, call Mrs. Stevens or Nola for me. Poor little Alison must be sedated and locked up for her own protection."

"Why, she's no more deranged than I am!" Mrs. Lowell stated. "For heaven's sake be sensible for a change!"

"Mrs. Lowell," the doctor warned, "if you keep on this way, I may find you unbalanced also. I suggest you go back into the front room and stay there. Oh, there you are, Honoria."

Honoria gave one look at the captive Alison and color flamed in her face. There was triumph as well as malevolence in her glare. "Do as Doctor says, Mrs. Lowell," she ordered.

Mrs. Lowell cast an apologetic and shame-faced glance at Alison, then turned and went into the front room.

Alison had given up trying to free herself from the doctor's surprisingly strong hold on her—she was only hurting her already sore arm and it seemed undignified to struggle. However, she hadn't expected to be treated like a mad dog with the doctor and Honoria on either side of her and Nola bringing up the rear.

She remembered Joe's warning about being careful and not rocking the boat. Oh, well, she could never sit still in a boat.

"There," the doctor said, "she's smiling. It's typical, you know, of psychotics. Smiles keep coming and going on their faces with no relevance to what's going on. We'll put her in her room and, after I've finished with the other patients, I'll spend some time with her. We won't give her a shot yet. I want her awake when I examine her. There, dear girl, here you are in your own cozy room again. Try to rest and I'll see you later."

The doctor then spoke to Nola as if Alison were not present. "It's a good thing her room is on the second floor. She can't escape from the window. We'll lock her in, and if she becomes violent, we'll have to put her"—he stopped and took a deep breath—"you know where."

The three custodians left Alison, closing and locking the door behind them, feeling undoubtedly that they'd been efficient wardens.

They didn't know Alison Munro!

Chapter Twelve

Alison wasted no time on despair. Her
mind worked briskly. She knew she had
to escape and she wanted to take
Gertrude with her. There was only one
safe way to do it, but first she had to make
a getaway from her room.

It was an old-fashioned room in an old-
fashioned house and the keys were just
as dated. It all depended on whether the
key to her room would still be in the keyhole. It probably would be because not
only the doctor but Nola, and maybe Rose,
might want entry.

She knelt by the door and peered

153

through the keyhole. There was no light striking her eye, and she hoped that meant the key was there. Alison had seen in movies, and read in books, the simple procedure of getting an outside key into a room. The problem, and it seemed dire, was that she had no paper to slide under the door so that the key would fall on it, allowing her to pull it through.

She had note paper but even an unfolded sheet would be so small, the key, when she pushed it out, had little chance of landing on it. What to do? A pillowcase? She tried it, but it was too soft and pleated itself. She needed something thin but stiff. If only she had a newspaper. The bath mat was too thick to slide under the door, and a clothes hanger was too risky.

An idea! The paper that lined the bureau drawers! Alison removed one sheet of it, tried it for size, stiffness, and slickness, and decided it would do. Now to plan. The sooner she made her move, the better. She should do it when everybody was busy but before the doctor had finished his rounds.

When she was out of her room, how was

she to get downstairs without being seen?
The dingy, narrow, seldom-used back
stairs might be safe. All right then, how
to get to the cellar, rescue Gertrude, and
flee to Fairview? That would pose a problem, but perhaps she could sneak out of
the nursing home, then go to the place on
the cliffs where she could climb down. If
the tide was low, she could get to the cave.
Then further planning could take place
at leisure.

She flew to the ocean-side window. The
tide was down now but seemed to be ris-
ing. She had to escape now—at once—
this minute!

Quickly Alison changed her skirt for a
pair of slacks and put on sneakers. She
kept on her sweater.

Her ear to the door told her nobody
was nearby, and she pushed the paper
under the door. Then—with an emory
board through the keyhole—she pressed
gently until she heard the key dropping
to the floor. She held her breath in a
silent prayer as she pulled the sheet of
paper toward her.

Success! In a second Alison had unlocked her door, peered into the hall, then relocked the empty room, leaving the key in the keyhole to confound her discoverer, and tiptoed to the back stairs.

There were voices coming from the kitchen. Making a cautious descent, she got to the bottom, then had to wait. Nancy, the cook, was berating Rose, and Sam was twitting Nola about something.

"Well, it's *your* job, not mine," Nola said, "and I have to take this to the doctor. Right now."

Alison could hear the nurse depart.

Then Sam's voice made her cringe. "I don't see why it's always me who has to take stuff to Gertrude. Always at night when I'd like to sleep for a change."

Rose said, "Well, stupid, night is the only time Gertrude is awake, as you very well know. The doctor has changed night into day for her. At least it leaves your days free."

"Free! You gotta be kidding. You think it's free to be sent to fetch that hellcat, Alison? For two cents I'd—" He lowered his voice, and in a tone just above a whisper, he added, "How she got out of that laundry room the other night I'll never know! I locked it securely, and it was locked when I went back to see if she was breathing. It was empty! At least I think it was—the light was so dim, I couldn't really see. Maybe she was hiding under one of the tubs—or in one. I should of looked. Oh, well, she's under lock and key now."

Alison thanked her lucky stars she had managed to pull the grate back over the drain when she'd gone down it. The laundry room's darkness had evidently hidden the rope tied to the tubs' stand.

"Anyway," Rose said, "you're paid a whale of a lot. I only wish I got half as much, and I work twice as hard!"

"Isn't it time for you to take trays around, Rose?" the cook asked. "We've had enough of this bickering. The doctor will probably stay for lunch, and that means more work for me. Sam, go get the doctor's favorite wine."

Alison could hear Rose depart with a tray, and then the slam of the cellar door meant that Sam had gone down to the wine shelves. Only Nancy, the cook, remained, and Alison must take her chance now to escape through the back door. She peered into the kitchen. Nancy had her back to her and was stirring something on the stove. The smell of food made Alison hungry, but she mustn't let her appetite spoil things.

She advanced a step, then backed up when Nancy turned. Alison advanced again and was thankful to see the cook disappear into the pantry.

As quiet and as quick as a mouse, Alison reached the back door and slipped through. Now she had to be equally furtive as she headed for the cliff. In her favor was the fact that lunch would absorb most of the patients, and the staff would be busy serving it or eating their own meals.

She ran to a clump of bushes, rested for a minute, then ran to another small copse of shrubs. Each time she paused, she was closer to the cliff edge, but shortly there was going to be a long run in the clear with no bush or tree to conceal her. Alison knew exactly which part of the cliff held her secret pathway. Her hands would get cut up again and her clothes torn, but once on the way down, she'd be safe—that was if the tide hadn't come in too far.

When she arrived, breathless, at her destination above the cliff's footholds, she looked back at the nursing home. There was someone on the front porch who seemed to be scanning the horizon, then looking in her direction.

Without another moment's hesitation, Alison let herself down, feeling with her foot for the first hole and keeping her head low. If the person, man or woman, had seen her, he must now believe he'd seen a mirage, or that his eyes needed examining.

When Alison had descended ten or twelve feet—and, oh, how slowly she was going!—she looked down at the incoming tide. What would she do—what *could* she do—if the waves started beating against the rocks before she reached the place where the ascent to the cave began? She was in danger here. Had she been foolish to flee from the nursing home? What would the doctor have done to her if she'd stayed? He would have had her doped, probably locked up in an inescapable place. He would have diagnosed her as crazy, and she had a horrid feeling he might have made advances to her. No, no matter what danger she faced here on the cliffside, it was a preferable danger!

She must hurry, hurry! The tide was advancing fast and her descent was slow. At last she reached the bottom, then saw there was no more than a foot of sand between the cliff and the ocean. Part of the sand was already covered, and waves were coming closer, closer, closer.

She had very few minutes to get to where she could see the white projection that was near the cave.

Running was like a nightmare—legs not properly functioning and all her efforts for speed in vain. Her feet acted as though they were glued to the sand, and each one had to be pulled up with force.

A wave struck Alison, not quite knocking her down, but making itself felt. Then came another lethal wave and another.

She was completely soaked and near collapse when the white projection was above her.

She reached for the first handhold and grasped it just as a huge wave was about to engulf her. She clung to the cliff while the wave receded, sucking at her, and carefully made her way to the cave.

She was cold and hurting. Very slowly she pushed herself up and up and up. Was her father's sleeping bag still in the back? It was, she saw upon reaching the cave, and so was a paper sack. Painfully she crawled to the sack. To her extreme pleasure, she found a piece of cheese and four stale doughnuts. Never had food tasted so good, and Alison ate all but one doughnut. The desire to crawl into the sleeping bag was almost overwhelming, but she knew she had a duty to perform first.

Quick, before her weary body took control, she must tug on the rope that still hung out of the opening from which she'd catapulted into the midst of the three men, to test it for strength. It was still solidly tied and now she had to face the exertion of hauling herself up.

Couldn't she wait until she'd slept a bit? No, definitely not. Gertrude was left alone during the daytime because she was always tranquilized, so Alison must make her move *now* while there would be no interference, while there was light.

She did a few deep bends and some pushups. She flexed her arm muscles and dried her sneakers on the paper sack. The action she was planning was "rocking the boat," wasn't it? Well, if her father and Joseph and Toby were so elusive, so dilly-dallying, action was up to her. There was only so much a prisoner could stand, and Alison believed that the nurse's cries for help had become weaker. Certainly they sounded more hopeless.

When she had been locked in the laundry room and Gertrude's cries had been suddenly hushed, and Alison's shouts unanswered, she had no doubt that Sam's large hand had been slapped over Gertrude's mouth.

No, she mustn't postpone her effort a moment longer. It was midafternoon or perhaps later. She took a deep breath and faced her task. The chime of a buoy sounded like a melancholy dirge, and Alison hoped it wasn't tolling for *her*.

Chapter Thirteen

Alison found it was much more difficult to haul herself up the drain than it had been to come down it. Her sore muscles protested every inch of the way. She forced herself onward, her heart pumping, her lungs straining, her legs aching.

After an eternity, she found herself on the floor of the laundry room. She lay there, every joint aching, every muscle quivering, and all the old bruises throbbing. What was she doing here? she asked herself. Why was she putting up with all the physical torture her mission involved? Was she Gertrude's guardian angel?

163

Not having an answer to any of her questions, she raised herself up, careful not to groan too loudly. Once she was on her feet, she tested the door.

It was shut but not locked.

On tiptoe, Alison went along the cellar until she reached the door with the shiny knob. What if she'd been mistaken? What if behind the door she found one of the staff?

What if Gertrude—oh, stop! she scolded herself. As if she didn't have enough troubles without inventing more!

There was a key in the door. Alison turned it and it quietly opened. There was some light streaming in from a big barred window, and Alison saw she hadn't made a mistake.

Gertrude's prison was dingy. There was a lumpy cot, stained walls, a rug so worn, the cording showed through the pile. There was a rickety table with a lamp on it and an old chair that wasn't very straight. Those were all the furnishings.

On the cot huddled a figure whose breathing was labored.

"Gertrude," Alison said quietly.

"Gertrude, wake up! I've come to get you out of here."

Gertrude moaned softly but didn't wake up.

Alison gently shook the woman's shoulder. "Come, dear! We've got to hurry. We mustn't lose any time. You must be away from your prison before Sam comes."

The word "Sam" seemed to penetrate, and Gertrude turned toward Alison. Her hair was a limp pepper and salt, which Alison remembered as being a crisp auburn. Her skin was the color of milk, and Alison knew it had been pink and quite pretty. Her eyes, when they opened to stare at Alison, seemed to water with despair.

"Can you get up, Gertrude?" Alison asked. "Here, I'll help."

The woman was very unsteady on her feet. She wobbled and had to sit down heavily on her bed. Her eyes were still quite unfocused and she obeyed Alison without any knowledge of what was happening.

Alison gave her a drink of water from a smeared glass that stood on the table.

That seemed to make her more alive.

"Oh—" Gertrude's voice was a hoarse whisper.

"I'm Alison Munro, don't you remember? We used to talk together. I'm here to rescue you. Can you understand, dear? I'm going to take you from your prison. But we've got to get going! Let's see you take a few steps."

Gertrude's tranquilizer was not easy to shake off, but a few more sips of water and a steadied pacing of the room began to help a bit.

"Have you any clothes, Gertrude?" Alison asked.

She saw that the woman was wearing flannel pajamas. There were slippers by the cot and a bathrobe was flung over the iron bedstead.

Gertrude shook her head and looked confused, as if it were her fault she had no wardrobe.

"It doesn't matter, dear. Here, I'll help you on with your robe and you put your feet in the slippers."

It was like talking to a very small child.

"All right, now we'll go! Ready?" Alison asked. She tried to be brisk and energetic,

but her own tiredness was hard to overcome.

With Gertrude hanging heavily on one
arm, Alison opened the door, got them both
through, and relocked it. This time she
did not leave the key in the keyhole. Let
Sam unravel that small fact.

Weaving and wobbling, the pair of them
got to the laundry room. How was Alison
going to persuade Gertrude to go down
the drain? And even if she could, how was
she to keep the woman from slipping and
injuring herself?

While she pondered this, she leant
Gertrude up against the tubs and took the
key from outside the door. Then she softly
closed and locked the door from the inside.
Let Sam wonder about *that,* too!

The key was in the keyhole in case she
ever (heaven forbid) had to get into the
house again by way of the drain. The key
to Gertrude's prison she put in a laundry
tub.

Alison was pleased to see the light of
intelligence begin to shine in Gertrude's
eyes. The sedation was gradually wearing
off.

Alison explained what they had to do

and Gertrude's eyes opened wide in alarm. Then a change came over the nurse and she smiled a faint smile. In an unused voice, she said she'd do whatever she had to do. Anything was better than being in a prison, even falling off the cliff after sliding down the drain.

Alison reassured her and hauled up the rope. She tied it securely around the nurse's waist and helped her into the drain. Alison then wrapped the rope around both her wrists and let it out gradually as the nurse descended.

Although Gertrude was rail thin, her weight was almost too much for Alison's trembling arms. When at last the rope hung loose and Alison knew that Gertrude had arrived in the cave, she did a few more deep bends and shoulder twists to limber herself up and then pulled her torn sweater down over her hands.

Her fingers were too raw to slow down her descent and she hoped the woolly sweater would keep her from being flung down the drain like an uncontrolled missile. She didn't need any more wounds, thank you.

Butterflies were busily churning in her stomach. What was the matter with her? Had all her hard-won courage been left behind? Had she used up every ounce of grit? She was so tired—so very, very tired.

But she kept forcing herself to go downward, downward, this time moving feet first.

When her sneakers were dangling in air and she knew she'd arrived, she felt strong arms grab her hips. Gertrude? It couldn't be!

It wasn't. When Alison had been gently moved out of the opening and set on her feet, she saw it was Joe who had helped her.

She rushed into his waiting arms and burst into sobs. He talked softly, and when her tears were spent, he slipped a handkerchief into her hand and told her to blow her nose.

"You've been rocking the boat again, haven't you, darling?"

She nodded guiltily. "But I rescued Gertrude!" she added proudly. "Nobody else was doing it, so I had to!"

She looked around and saw that

Gertrude was lying on the sleeping bag, not asleep but not very wide awake either.

"Were you here when Gertrude slid down the drain?" Alison asked Joe.

"I almost died of shock, I can tell you," he answered. "Here was a complete stranger sliding into this very private cave, not saying a word, looking like a ghost, and scared to death. I didn't know what to think, what to say, what to do. I finally pointed to the sleeping bag. So this is Gertrude?"

Alison nodded again. "I—I think I'll join her on the sleeping bag. I can't stay awake any longer. You don't have any food with you, do you? And just what are you doing here anyway?"

"I'm waiting for the others so we can finalize our plans. We were to meet here at six. They're late."

"Daddy will be here?"

"Yes, darling. Toby, too."

"But the tide is high. Nobody can get here except at low tide. How—?"

"There are ways, dear. Will you accept my offer?" Joe said.

"You haven't made one yet."

"Oh, so I haven't. Well, it'll wait. Go to sleep now. I'll wake you when it's necessary."

"First I'll share the one remaining doughnut with Gertrude."

"Sorry, love, I ate it."

"Toad! Hog!" Alison said.

"Do not jest with your superior in his hour of need," Joe said.

"I'm too tired to figure out your quaint figures of speech," Alison said, yawning.

She went to the back of the cave and lay down with the already sleeping nurse. She felt secure and comfortable with Joe nearby. He followed her and covered them both with the voluminous jacket he had been wearing.

"Sleep, my beauty," he said softly.

Voices woke Alison up.

"Daddy?" she cried and was shortly smothered in her father's warm embrace.

"Dr. Lansing has told me of your brave deeds, Lis," he said. "You've been wonderful, albeit foolhardy."

"Dr. Lansing?" Alison exclaimed. "Is Joe a doctor? A doctor of what?"

"Joe is a general practitioner," her father continued, "and I've persuaded him to come to Aiken when all this mess is cleared up. Will you be glad?"

Alison was dazed. Joe a doctor!

"Joseph is in on this investigation," her father said, "at my behest. Toby is on his own, but he's joined up with us. Oh, here he comes now!"

Toby came into the cave as if no climbing or avoiding tides had been faced. How in the world was it done? Alison wondered.

Joe grinned wickedly at her. "I told you, darling, that there were ways of getting to the cave."

Alison looked at him with something less than affection. What an irritating man! How she loved him even so!

She greeted Toby and pointed to Gertrude, who was still asleep.

"*I* rescued her," Alison said proudly.

The reunion between the newly awakened Gertrude and her nephew, Toby, was touching. There were tears on both sides.

Alison's father told Gertrude he was happy to see her again and that she'd be an important witness. Gertrude was alarmed and asked if she would have to face the doctor, Nola, Honoria, and Sam again. She showed fear and only Toby's steadying arm and soothing words calmed her.

At last she said, "I'll be a witness. I'll— I'll tell all about—I'll—"

"There, there," Toby said. "We'll be with you all the time. Don't worry. Alison will be a witness and so will I, dear Aunt Gertrude."

"Daddy," Alison said, "there are so many questions I need to ask. Like who was it I buried thinking it was you? And what kept you away? And why is Joe helping you? And how the heck do you get into this cave without—without—"

"First things first, darling," Joe said. "Mr. Munro will answer everything later, but right now we all have to go to the Honoria Nursing Home where we know the doctor is enjoying his last bout of power. Gertrude, are you up to going with us?"

"Anything," Gertrude said with determination.

"All right. Alison, follow me."

Joe led the way out of the cave. He made an abrupt turn to the right, into a concealed crevice. Just out of sight was a sturdy ladder going up to the top of the cliff and hidden above by a large bush.

All I went through, Alison thought bitterly, and here was the perfectly easy exit and entrance! No tide to bother with, no cuts, no bruises, no drain!

Chapter Fourteen

Alison knew that to the end of her life she would never forget the big scene in the front room at the home.

When the group from the cave entered the room, they had a momentarily paralyzing effect on Dr. Luther Pitt. His complexion rapidly assumed the hue of a turkey wattle.

Mrs. Lowell, looking at Alison in her torn garb, said, "Great heavens!"

Honoria seemed possessed by an uncontrollable gaiety that bordered on hysteria, and her eyes were wild as she tried to pretend a welcome for the newcomers.

175

She bared her teeth without smiling.

The benumbed doctor's attention was riveted on Gertrude. "How—how—" he stuttered, "how n-nice to see you, my dear!"

"Oh, goody," Mrs. Lowell said with a wink at Alison, "here comes Miss Thermometer. Now we are complete."

Toby stood tall and started talking. "You will remember," he said, "there was a missing bouillon cup from Mr. Newman's room. I took it. I took it and had the remains of the broth analyzed."

He looked around at three stricken faces that tried to look indifferent. "The poison was antimony salts, effective from forty-eight hours to three or four days. Undetectable taste and odor when placed in bouillon. The doctor knows all about that, don't you, Dr. Pitt? Antimony—its compounds are used in medicines."

Joseph Lansing now took up the stand, so to speak. "You talk of Dr. Pitt. A generous euphemism, Toby. Luther Pitt's license to practice has never been suspended surprisingly." He paused dramatically. "Because he never *had* a license!"

Luther Pitt spluttered vindications of himself, his career, his honest work, growing redder and redder in the face.

Alison's father took the accusing stand now. "I believe," he said quietly, "that the hoodwinking, defrauding, pretend Dr. Luther Pitt soon will be drawing a set of numbered coveralls from supplies at some prison."

"Now look here, my good fellow," Pitt said, trying desperately to present a calm appearance, "you have no right to come into this honorable nursing home disturbing the patients and—"

"Of course, we all know that the home is unlicensed too," Mr. Munro said. "To get a license, the home would have to be inspected, and you couldn't take that chance. Could you, Honoria?" He suddenly turned to the big woman.

She was as pale as the doctor was purple. "I—I don't know what you're talking about," she said, her voice squeaking with alarm.

"I think you do," Joe said. "Mr. Munro and I have discovered that Luther Pitt is a genial crook. His alias is Herbert Sen-

ton. He's quite well known by the police
in other states. We also know how many
of your patients were conned into willing
their estates to you. And we know that
many were given the dose of antimony.
No, don't try to escape! The house is sur-
rounded by police. And you might as well
give up willingly. We have Gertrude Smith
as a witness to your nefarious practices.
The staff has already been nabbed. Sam,
too, you'll be glad to hear, Gertrude!"

"I can't believe this is happening to me,"
Luther Pitt or Herbert Senton whined.

"To *you!*" screamed Honoria. "It's *my*
nursing home that's going to be closed,
not *yours!*"

"Who said anything about closing the
home?" Joe asked quietly. "We are going
to keep it open with young Toby Weston
as manager, Gertrude as head nurse. And
we will see to it that a whole new staff
and a reputable doctor are assigned. So,
Mrs. Lowell, you and Mr. Keene and the
remaining bed patients are free to stay or
go as you wish. Incidentally, the bed patients will probably be joining you for
meals now, and there will be no more doc-
tored bouillon served."

"Oh, how lovely!" Honoria gushed with a smile like that of a hungry crocodile. "Oh, how glad I am to hear that! I'll be so happy to go along with your plans!"

"Mental myopia," Joe said, looking pityingly at Honoria. "I believe incurable. No, dear lady, you and your boyfriend, Pitt, will be indicted, jailed, and dishonored. Nola and Sam will serve sentences and perhaps the rest of the staff will receive only reprimands. And now, you may pack what you need. I'll tell the police you are ready."

Toby and Gertrude stayed at the home, both of them full of plans and happy bustle. A new cook would be sent if Nancy left. Rose begged to keep her job, saying she "never did nothing bad to no one."

Alison and her father and Joseph planned to meet at the cottage in Fairview. Alison's car had been made usable and she took pleasure in having her wheels once more. Her exhaustion had miraculously disappeared when Joseph said he had something to ask her. She was quite ready to accept.

When all three met at the cottage, Alison wanted answers from her father.

"Who did I bury in the family plot, Daddy? I thought it was you because he wore your ring and your pajamas."

"An old school chum, Lis. Poor fellow was dying and was willing to take my place in the home so I could follow up leads regarding Pitt's villainy. His ring was his own because we both went to the same school. His pajamas were mine because I gave them to him. We had always looked rather alike. And with the dim light in his room, no wonder you were fooled. I'm terribly sorry I caused you pain, dear, but it seemed worth it to get rid of the criminals. Will you forgive me? And now I'll let you and Dr. Lansing have a bit of privacy. See you later."

Joe sat next to Alison. She looked him up and down without enthusiasm. At least that was the impression she wished to convey. She mustn't be forward, she told herself.

"Why are you holding yourself so stiffly, darling?" Joe asked.

"I'm afraid I might clutch at you," Alison responded shyly. "Mother always said one should never clutch. It makes men nervous."

"Make me nervous!"

It was a laughing, joyous kiss that followed. Alison believed it was definitely the nicest kiss she'd ever received.

Frampton, who had instantly made himself at home, looked up and wagged his tail. His two favorite people were together and looked as if they were going to stay that way.